What people are saying...

"This makes it so easy to build your vocabulary through reading! I majored in English and as a word lover myself, I recognized many of the words in this book but still found myself looking at the definitions that were provided just to be sure I understood their meaning. Especially with all of the dumbed-down and questionable literature being published for young adults these days, such a series has tremendous potential to actually enhance their knowledge while upholding positive moral values."

—Teri Ann Berg Olsen, *Knowledge House*

"Burk's style is easy for the reader and geared to teenagers in the high school years. This book has 300 words that, for the most part, will be new to the reader... What an incredible way to increase the writing and speaking skills of your student!"

—Jennifer Barker, *The Old Schoolhouse Magazine*

"There are very few better ways to quickly read and actually remember 300 high-level words, such as "ruminate," "lachrymose," "salubrious" and "pulchritude." Some of the words may be recognized by many readers, but even this reader was learning new words throughout."

—Chloe O'Connor, *The Signal*

"Besides being an excellent tool to enhance vocabulary and language development, pre-teens and teens will find the story engaging. Best of all, the story steers clear of offensive language and unsavory themes."

—Anne Gebhart, *Heart of Texas*

D1110532

Books in VocabCafé Series

The $ummer
of $aint Nick

By Josh Burk

Maven of Memory Publishing
Hurst, Texas

The Summer of Saint Nick

Copyright © 2007, 2012 by Maven of Memory Publishing
Hurst, Texas

ISBN 978-0-9768042-2-2
LCCN 2007907900

The VocabCafé Book Series is intended to encourage the study and investigation of the English language. This book is not, nor does it purport itself to be, the complete and final authority on word usage and definitions. Maven of Memory Publishing is not responsible for any errors, omissions, or misunderstandings contained in this book or derived from information contained herein.

Cover and layout by impact studios

Printed in the United States of America

To my friend and Savior, Jesus Christ, without whom I could neither create nor be anything.

An Introduction to VocabCafé

The purpose of the VocabCafé book series is to encourage the development of vocabulary knowledge. At Maven of Memory Publishing we believe that a good understanding of vocabulary words is crucial to lifelong success. Contained inside this novella are more than 300 words that can be helpful in improving the vocabulary of any reader, which can lead to better reading, writing, and speaking skills. It can also help improve test scores for students intending to take standardized exams.

Every vocabulary word is placed in the context of a narrative story. The storyline and sentences surrounding the words should help readers easily deduce their meanings. For easy reference and instant reinforcement, the literal definitions of every word are at the bottom of each page. At the end of each chapter there is a review of the vocabulary words featured in that section. We recommend that you go over this word review immediately after finishing the chapter in order to study the definitions while their context remains fresh.

These books were written with an intended audience of high school teenagers, although many parents find them appropriate for younger students. As a family-based company, our goal is to make a quality product that can be enjoyed by everyone. These stories contain no magic, sorcery, swear words, or illicit situations. Nonetheless, we recommend that parents read every book (not just ours) that they give their children to make sure the messages and themes coincide with their beliefs and standards.

Accompanying flash cards organized by chapter are available for purchase and highly recommended to help ensure success. Each card has the word definition and its use in the story. Reviewing these will help you in your quest for mastery of vocabulary words.

We hope this series is instrumental in helping you advance your proficiency with the English language.

Good Luck!
The VocabCafé Team

The $ummer
of $aint Nick

1

The summer sun attracted Nick's attention. He gazed through the classroom windows. Outside was freedom. Mr. Schlipp, his teacher, continued with his boring, *soporific* lectures—even though finals had already been taken. No one was listening. In ten minutes, terribly disappointing tenth grade would be over.

Nick Franklin was one of those all-star students every mom wanted her daughter to marry and every daughter wanted her mom to quit talking about. Smart, studious, and courteous—he had everything he needed to become an amazing lawyer, just like he wanted...but he couldn't get a girlfriend. His appearance presented the biggest problem. Nick was below average in height, blind without his wide-rimmed glasses, and exceptionally poor at sports.

Teachers loved him, though. He was always willing to answer questions and volunteer to help with demonstrations. This gung-ho *alacrity*, however, isolated Nick from his classmates.

Through the window, Nick saw freedom from all the experiences that had made high school disastrous. The summer could help him forget football, basketball, track,

Soporific	(soh-puh-**rif**-ik) – ADJ – causing or tending to cause sleep
Alacrity	(uh-**lak**-ri-tee) – N – cheerful readiness or willingness

and wrestling try-outs. He could forget accidentally calling his homeroom teacher "Mommy." And, most importantly, he could forget the fact that he hadn't made any friends the entire year—not one.

The rustling of books and backpacks brought Nick back to reality. The bell hadn't yet rung, but students were already clearing their desks and standing up. "Well, I know you aren't listening, but I hope you all have a good summer," said the frustrated Mr. Schlipp. On those words, the class was dismissed a few minutes early. Nick packed his stuff and left the room.

In the hallway, he was stopped by the *pugnacious* Ryan Finley, a guy who received special joy from bullying and fighting. (We all have our hobbies.) "Nicholas," Ryan said, "I've been thinking a lot about our interactions lately. I know sometimes I can be mean, so I bought you this soda to make amends." As he handed it to Nick, Ryan popped the top and sprayed soda all over Nick's pants. At that moment, the bell rang and the hallway was instantly filled with students laughing at the mishap. Nick had to make a crucial, defining decision: stay and fight like a man, or run away.

He made a break for the front doors. If he didn't escape fast, the nickname "Nick Pee-Pants" would easily become a *demotic* phrase in the regular conversations of Bloomington High School. Ryan, and other kids, too, made it a hateful game to taunt him with cruel nicknames and *besmirch* his reputation.

Pugnacious	(puhg-**ney**-shuhs) – ADJ – taking pleasure in hostility
Demotic	(dih-**mot**-ik) – ADJ – popular; vernacular; of or pertaining to common speech
Besmirch	(bi-**smurch**) – V – to soil; tarnish: discolor; to detract from the luster

Past the flagpole, past the bus, as he got farther and farther away from the school, his run slowed to an **amble**. Fortunately, in the small town of Bloomington, Kansas, most things were within walking distance.

Today, Nick was not walking home. He was going to an old farmhouse on the outskirts of town. It had been deserted years ago. Nick found it once during an attempt to run away from home. When he was nine, his father abandoned the family. During that difficult time, the farmhouse became Nick's place of solitude. He called it "The Penthouse," a name he painted on a sign and hung on the door. Inside, he kept his law books, sleeping bag, and the rest of his prized **accouterments**.

The road toward his penthouse was made of dirt. It used to be in the farmers' district of town, but after a seven-year drought, most of the farmers had moved away. There were just a few lonely people left, all of whom knew Nick by name. He was regularly greeted by them every time he walked down the street.

Nick passed by a familiar house and saw Mrs. Eugenia Ray sitting in her rocking chair, fanning herself. The blind widow's head perked up at the sound of his footsteps, so he made his presence known. "Afternoon, Mrs. Ray."

"Son, come up here," she called. After a pause, she said, "The heat always gives me such problems these summer months, but I know there's something bothering you not related to the weather." Even though Mrs. Ray was blind, she seemed able to "see" things others didn't because of her **clairvoyant** sensitivities.

Amble	(**am**-buhl) – N – a leisurely walk
Accouterments	(uh-**koo**-ter-muhnts) – N – equipment, trappings
Clairvoyant	(klair-**voi**-uhnt) – ADJ – having the power of seeing objects or actions beyond the natural range of vision

"It doesn't matter," said Nick. "I'm going to go to college and get out of this crummy town."

"The Lord will take care of your problems," she replied. "You just got to wait. Everything will happen in its time. You can't run away. And I think you've run a bit today already."

Nick smiled. Mrs. Ray was God's biggest advocate, and she never failed to speak her mind. She was known to make *delphic* predictions about the future that were unclear at first, but always had a way of coming true in the long run.

Mrs. Ray got up from the chair and patted down her flower-pattern dress. "I'm going to get some lemonade for us both to cool down with."

She went inside her small country house and pulled out a pitcher from the icebox. "I figured you'd be stopping by today, so I made this earlier." She placed the pitcher on her pink table cloth that *quaintly* matched the curtains and the old-fashioned wallpaper. She got out the glasses and filled them up.

Mrs. Ray came back out to the front porch with a glass in each hand. "You enjoy this now, because God made lemonade to remind us that even lemons can be a wonderful thing."

Nick and Mrs. Ray drank in silence, allowing the cool drink to *ameliorate* the heat. When Nick was finished, he excused himself. "Thanks for the lemonade, Mrs. Ray, but I have some reading I'd like to do. I really appreciate it," he said, then began walking off the porch.

Delphic	(**del**-fik) – ADJ – oracular; obscure; ambiguous
Quaintly	(**kweynt**-lee) – ADV – in a beautifully old-fashioned way
Ameliorate	(uh-**meel**-yuh-reyt) – V – to make more tolerable; to make easier

"You know you're welcome here anytime!" She waved good-bye.

Nick resumed the leisurely stroll to his penthouse. When he went there, the one thing he enjoyed most was walking through the *bucolic* landscape of the countryside. Trees, grass, and flowers—everything made him glad to be alive. He would gaze into the sky and his problems would just fly away.

By the time he reached the penthouse, it was late in the afternoon, but there was still plenty of time before the sun would go down. Nick entered the house and went straight to his library, where he had spent many evenings reading law books. His house had four rooms in all: the library, kitchen, bedroom, and game room—all of which Nick had assigned when he was much younger. Nick grabbed *An Introduction to Property Law* and sat in his favorite corner. He liked to read there *ensconced* in the snug spot because light streamed in from the western window in the afternoon.

He became lost in his book, imagining himself as a big-shot lawyer in a big city. He thought of the hot red Ferrari he was going to buy, along with all the cool gadgets and toys that only wealth can afford. Someday Nick wanted to come back to Bloomington and buy his penthouse. It was his place of *repose,* where he could always find a peaceful refuge. He dreamed of the future until he noticed something shocking that pertained to his life in the present.

"Wow!" he exclaimed. "That would be amazing!"

He marked the page and shut the book.

Bucolic	(byoo-**kol**-ik) – ADJ – typically rural
Ensconce	(en-**skons**) – V – to settle snugly or securely
Repose	(ree-**pohz**) – N – peace or tranquility

WORD REVIEW

Accouterments
Alacrity
Amble
Ameliorate
Besmirch

Bucolic
Clairvoyant
Delphic
Demotic
Ensconce

Pugnacious
Quaintly
Repose
Soporific

2

The sun had begun to set, and Nick knew it was time for him to go to his real home. His mom, who worked as a nurse, would be getting off work, and Nick didn't want her to worry.

The *tortuous* road toward town always seemed longer on the way back home—maybe because Nick always took the scenic route, past Second Bloomington Church, through Peabody Park, and alongside the hardware store. By the time he reached his actual *domicile*, it was 7:20 p.m., and Sarah Franklin, his mom, was already home.

Nick walked through the front door of their small duplex. "Mom, I'm home!" He walked over to his mother, who was seated on the sofa, and kissed her on the top of her forehead.

"Hi, honey, how was your last day of school?"

"Uh, it wasn't so good," he responded.

"I'm sorry, baby…I brought home some chicken. It's in the fridge if you want it."

Nick went into the kitchen and opened the refrigerator. He pulled out the big paper box of chicken legs and began to choose the most desirable pieces. He took one of his mom's blue and white duck-patterned china plates

Tortuous	(**tawr**-choo-uhs) – ADJ – winding; twisted
Domicile	(**dom**-uh-sahyl) – N – place of residence

from the cabinet and placed several fried legs on it.

They sat on the couch quietly eating their supper. Every night, Nick and his mom would watch several hours of game shows, talk shows, and dramas. When it was bedtime, Mrs. Franklin kissed Nick goodnight.

"What are your plans for tomorrow?" she asked. "Now that you're a free man and all."

"It's Saturday, Mom. I'm going to Mr. Bering's office, as always. I have something really exciting to ask him."

"What's that?"

"I'll tell you after I find out a little bit more," he responded.

Nick and his mom went to their separate bedrooms and fell asleep.

WORD REVIEW

Domicile
Tortuous

3

The Law Office of James Bering was located in the downtown square southwest of the courthouse. It was on the second floor of the historic McMillan building. Mr. Bering took special pride in understanding and applying *jurisprudence*; he loved everything about being a lawyer. He became fast friends with anyone interested in law.

For years, Mr. Bering had acted as Nick's mentor. Like clockwork, Nick would visit the office every Saturday morning, and the two would talk about law and school. Even though Mr. Bering specialized in law, he had a *sagacious* understanding of many other aspects of life as well.

Nick came into the office early, excited about his discovery. As he knocked on the door, Mr. Bering's voice rang out, "It's open! Come on in."

Mr. Bering was sitting at his desk. Papers were scattered all over the room. Nick tiptoed carefully across the carpet to avoid stepping on them.

"Walk all over those," Mr. Bering said. "If they're on the floor, I'm done with them."

"Working on a big case?" Nick asked. That could

Jurisprudence	(joo r-is-**prood**-ns) – N – the science or philosophy of law
Sagacious	(suh-**gey**-shuhs) – ADJ – having or showing acute mental discernment and keen practical sense; shrewd

generally be assumed when his office was this cluttered.

"I'm just going through some old records. But I'm glad you're here; I need a break from it anyway. What's up?"

Nick pulled up a chair, and the sound of paper crunching momentarily filled the room. "When I was reading yesterday, I discovered something called Adverse Possession. And I think I might qualify for it," Nick said.

"If you don't stop reading those law books," replied Mr. Bering, "you are not even going to need to go to Law School!" Nick grinned and Mr. Bering continued. "Here's how Adverse Possession works: when someone uses a property for so long without being stopped by the property owners, this person has the right of ownership of the property. The land owners, by not prohibiting the use of their property, *relinquish* their rights to it. There are a few qualifications that have to be met, though. Have you possessed the land for five years or longer?"

"Yes."

"Has your possession of the property been open and public?"

"Yes, I even have a sign on the front door."

"Have you ever received notice from the property owner of your illegal presence?"

"Never, not even once."

"Seriously? Where is this property? I mean, I don't want to get your hopes up, but I think we've got a good case!"

Suddenly a knock came at the door. Without waiting for a response, Celeste Bering, sixteen-year-old daughter of James and Nancy Bering, entered the room. Nick gulped and his palms grew clammy. Celeste was a dream. She had blond hair and blue eyes, wore a classy

---

Relinquish   (ri-**ling**-kwish) – V – to give up; surrender

dress, and, to put it plainly, looked like a model. For Nick, the beautiful Celeste was the perfect example of *pulchritude.* Ever since middle school, he'd had a secret crush on her. He was able, however, to **dissemble** an air of apathy, not wanting his intense feelings for her to be known, especially by Mr. Bering.

"Dad," Celeste said, "could you get me an interview with Judge Reinhorn? I'm working on a story that needs a legal expert."

"Why don't you use your father? I know a little something about law."

"If I'm going to be a serious journalist, I *cannot* use my father as an expert witness. Don't you think that's a little unprofessional?" After saying this, Celeste noticed Nick. "Oh, hey, Nick, how are you?"

Nick wasn't normally shy, but around Celeste…he was definitely *taciturn.*

"A. . .ah, hey," Nick responded weakly.

Celeste returned her attention to her father. "Anyway, if you could get me that interview, I would appreciate it." With that, she walked out of the room.

"How do you like that?" said Mr. Bering. "My only daughter has no need for her old man anymore, except to use for contact information." He cleared his throat. "Now about Adverse Possession: What we need to do is file an action to quiet title, which is basically a lawsuit requesting the rights to the property. If everything goes well, the property will be yours within the week. Now let's make a case."

Pulchritude	(**puhl**-kri-tood) – N – beauty; comeliness
Dissemble	(di-**sem**-buhl) – V – to conceal the real nature; to put on an appearance of
Taciturn	(**tas**-i-turn) – ADJ – inclined to silence; quiet

Nick began to tell Mr. Bering all about his penthouse and the property where it was located.

"It's some old farmer's land," he said. "All the neighbors say the guy's dead. I claimed it as a clubhouse when I was about nine, and I've been going there ever since."

"Here's what I'm going to do," Mr. Bering began. "I'm going to call Judge Reinhorn and set up a court date for you and an interview time for Celeste. Then I'm going to finish with these old papers. I'll call your house with the schedule of our lawsuit."

Nick could not contain his excitement. He gave Mr. Bering a slow grin, and then left his office with a spring in his step. It was as if everything were right with the world. The sky was bluer than blue, and in the air, Nick could smell the *redolent* flowers, trees, and homemade apple pies.

A car tire began to screech behind Nick. He turned sharply and watched as an old black Corvette speedily rolled up beside him and stopped. Nick groaned. It was Ryan Finley, whose meanness baffled Nick. Ryan's evil side must be completely **endogenous,** having no external factors causing it, since he had a father who was genuinely friendly and a super nice girlfriend, Misty Vaughn,

The tinted driver's side window rolled down, revealing Ryan's face. "Hey, buddy," Ryan said sarcastically. "I just wanted to let you know where the party is tonight. Everyone's going to the new drive-in to celebrate school ending. Bring your hot car and your nonexistent girlfriend, and just tell everyone that Ryan invited you. See ya there?"

Redolent   (**red**-l-uhnt) – ADJ – having a pleasant odor; fragrant
Endogenous   (en-**doj**-uh-nuhs) – ADJ – derived internally;
                      proceeding from within

Ryan gave Nick an exaggerated wink and sped away. His tires screeched at the end of the road, solely to symbolize his *puissance* by the power of his car. By this time, Nick's mood had turned around completely. Ryan's words served to completely **belittle** him, and he suddenly felt like a loser. Every step he took reminded him that he did not own a car and probably *would* not own one until after law school. He started to notice the weeds in the sidewalk and the broken-down playground next to the road. His city no longer looked like a wonderland, just a gross dump. The trees no longer had leaves and the lawns were no longer green. Everything around him was a disgusting shade of brown.

Nick was still **disconsolate** the next morning at church despite the bright sunshine of the new day. He and his mom had been going to Second Bloomington for years, as had nearly everybody else in town. People rarely missed a Sunday morning service—it was one of few towns still demonstrating such church-going commitment. Nick and his mom always sat in the same seats, second row farthest to the left. The pew *hassock* had their permanent indentations.

Reverend William Grey began the prayer requests. "There is a woman among our midst who is in the need of a babysitter for her two small children when she is working. Pray that the Lord will send someone her way...Brother Tommy is going to the hospital again to run some more

Puissance	(**pyoo**-uh-suhns) – N – power, might, or force
Belittle	(bih-**lit**-l) – V – to disparage; to make small
Disconsolate	(dis-**kon**-suh-lit) – ADJ – without hope; hopelessly unhappy
Hassock	(**has**-uhk) – N – a thick, firm cushion used as a footstool or for kneeling

tests. Pray that it will all come out clear…And as you all know, the Church's community center is going to close. Pray that all the people who were ministered by it can find somewhere else where they can enjoy community and the comfort of a family. While you are making those requests to our Father, Sister Jennifer Simms is going to come up here and sing 'It is Well with My Soul.'"

As Nick bowed his head and heard Sister Simms' soothing voice, he stopped feeling sorry for himself. There were other problems so much more significant than his own.

After the service, Nick was met outside by Mr. Bering and his family. "Hey, Nick," said Mr. Bering, "We got a court date this Tuesday morning. Be at my office at about eight a.m."

"I will definitely be there," said Nick.

His smile returned.

WORD REVIEW

Belittle   Hassock   Redolent
Disconsolate   Jurisprudence   Relinquish
Dissemble   Puissance   Sagacious
Endogenous   Pulchritude   Taciturn

4

Tuesday morning Nick woke up early, despite the fact that he could barely sleep the night before. Today would be a dream come true. He could gain ownership of the penthouse and also get some courtroom experience. The *levity* of his buoyant soul was indescribable.

His mom knocked on the door. She opened it cautiously. In her hands was a brand new pin-striped suit. "I was saving this for your birthday, but I think you could better use it now," she said.

Nick jumped out of bed, grabbed the suit, and gave her a huge hug. He went to his mirror and began to try the jacket on over his pajamas. *This is perfect,* he thought. *I'm going to look like I belong there.*

His mom left him in peace, and Nick began getting ready. He eagerly looked over his notes with **unremitting** energy. He had pictures of the property and records of his longstanding occupancy, including a signed statement by Mrs. Eugenia Ray. After he read through the sections in his law books that covered Adverse Possession, he put on his nice new suit, took a final look in the mirror, and thought, *I'm ready.*

Levity	(**lev**-i-tee) – N – lightness of mind, character, or behavior
Unremitting	(uhn-ri-**mit**-ing) – ADJ – not stopping or slackening

At about seven thirty, Nick left his house with the ***glut*** of documents and headed toward the McMillan building.

"Wow, you're looking sharp," Mr. Bering said when Nick walked into the office. "Are you ready for our big day?"

"Ready as I'll ever be," responded Nick.

"You know that you'll almost definitely be put on the stand and questioned. You're going to have to fight for your right to this property."

"Well, I brought some stuff along to help my case." Nick handed his files to Mr. Bering.

"You really did your homework!" Mr. Bering exclaimed while sifting through the documents and photographs that Nick had brought. After discussing the information in detail, they both headed out the door for the courthouse.

The courtroom was already filled with people when Nick and Mr. Bering entered. There were many other cases on the schedule that day, and Nick and Mr. Bering would have to wait their turn. At exactly nine o'clock, the honorable Judge Reinhorn entered the room. Reinhorn was a big man and so was his reputation. His judgeship was an ***eminent*** role and he attended almost every political fundraiser and event in the community. He banged his gavel and said, "Court is now in session."

Several cases proceeded, and Nick watched them intently. He studied how the lawyers handled themselves and the evidence they had brought. These cases reassured him that his own would go fine, but this did not keep the butterflies from floating around in his stomach. He almost jumped out of his seat when the judge called out, "Adverse

Glut	(gluht) – N – a full supply
Eminent	(**em**-uh-nuhnt) – ADJ – high in station, rank, or repute

possession and quiet claim suit: will the parties Mr. Franklin, Mr. Bering, and Mr. McEntire please come to the front."

Nick was almost shaking as they approached the judge.

"Well, Mr. Bering and Mr. Franklin, it seems as though the deed holder, Mr. McEntire, failed to show up this morning for these proceedings. I hate to reward indifference and *indolence*, so I am very interested in awarding you this case. However, it does bother me that the plaintiff is a sixteen-year-old boy." Nick cringed. "Tell me, Mr. Franklin, being so young, how are you even able to file an Adverse Possession suit?"

Nick took a deep breath. "Well, sir, I have been going to this property since I was nine. I've spent a lot of time there, and I even keep my personal belongings in the building. I have pictures of the property and of myself there through the years." Nick handed Judge Reinhorn the pictures, and he looked at them with intrigue. "I also have a sworn statement written by a neighbor professing my open and public occupation." He handed the judge the statement.

"It looks as if everything is in order. It does appear that you, Mr. Franklin, have been a *denizen* of the property for the necessary period of time. And because no one came to oppose this suit for a quiet claim, I intend to award you legal ownership of this property. But before I do that, I want you to realize that this will require you to not only maintain the premises in a good working order as stated in the city ordinances, but also to pay the required taxes. Do you realize this, young man?"

"Yes, sir, and I am willing to take all the responsibility,"

Indolence   (**in**-dl-uhns) – N – the state of desiring to avoid exertion; laziness

Denizen   (**den**-uh-zuhn) – N – an inhabitant; resident

Nick replied.

The judge smiled. "Well all right then. I hereby award this property, in the county of Clarksville in the city of Bloomington, Kansas, to the plaintiff, Mr. Nick Franklin." He slammed his gavel, and the case was closed. Nick and Mr. Bering walked out of the courtroom triumphant.

"I didn't even have to say a thing! You were meant to be a lawyer, Nick," Mr. Bering *pontificated.*

"Thanks, Mr. Bering. I hope so," said Nick.

"I hope this proves to you that education and *erudition* pay off. To celebrate, why don't I take you out to lunch?"

"Thanks, but no thanks," Nick replied. "I think I'm going to go to the hospital and tell my mom the news. Then maybe I'll go to the hardware store. You heard the judge—I need to be making some repairs and cleaning up a little."

"You're beginning to sound just like the *proprietary* owner of the place."

They ended their conversation with a very professional handshake. Mr. Bering headed off to his office, while Nick went straight for the hospital. His mom worked in the Emergency Room, so upon arriving at the Clarksville County General Hospital, Nick walked toward the Emergency entrance. Several reasonably sick people waited to be admitted in the foyer; however, in this peaceful town there were very rarely any serious emergencies—mostly just broken limbs, unknown ailments, and sometimes hunting accidents.

Nick walked up to the receptionist, who gave him a

Pontificate	(pon-**tif**-i-keyt) – V – to speak in a pompous manner
Erudition	(er-yoo-**dish**-uhn) – N – acquired knowledge; scholarship
Proprietary	(pruh-**prahy**-i-ter-ee) – ADJ – characteristic of an owner

smile of recognition. "Hey, Nick," she said. "You're looking incredibly sharp today. I'll go see if your mom is available." The young lady pleasantly walked off in search of Nick's mom. After a few minutes, Sarah Franklin appeared from behind the other side. "Honey, how did it go?" She paused and looked at him. "You did great! I can just see it in your eyes" "Yeah," Nick said, "I got the property."

His mom shrieked and gave him a big hug. "I am *so* proud of you!" She looked him straight in the eyes. "I want to celebrate with you, but it will have to be tonight. There's a *dearth* of help around here and I'm needed badly," she said. "But I love you!" She waved goodbye and disappeared down the corridor of the emergency room floor.

Nick liked that his mom was a nurse. The fact that she was always helping people somehow *inured* him to the fact that she was often absent from home. When Nick was younger and she was just beginning her career, she had had to work strange hours, and the two of them barely got to see one another. As her seniority grew, she could make her schedule a lot more *diurnal,* which was a better match to his own schedule of school during the day and free time in the evening. She and Nick had plenty of opportunities to see one another now, and they both liked that.

Nick then wandered to the hardware store. He needed a machete to cut down the *inordinate* amount of weeds growing all over his property. He doubted that a city code enforcer would ever come close to checking to see

---

Dearth	(durth) – N – scarcity or scanty supply; lack
Inure	(in-**yoor**) – V – to toughen or harden; to become accustomed
Diurnal	(dahy-**ur**-nl) – ADJ – of or pertaining to each day; active by day (opposed to nocturnal)
Inordinate	(in-**awr**-dn-it) – ADJ – excessive; uncontrolled

whether or not he was in obedience, yet he felt a certain pride from the new responsibility of taking care of his own land. As he walked through the store looking for his machete, he noticed some other things that he could buy. *I could use some new paint,* he thought. *Oh, and some window cleaner would be useful...* As Nick walked through the aisles, he began to pick up more and more stuff: tools, decorations—even rat poison. He'd been saving money for a brand new featherweight mountain trekker, but house repair became an even more pressing need. He took a cart full of merchandise to check out. Two-hundred forty-four dollars and sixty-three cents later, Nick left the store.

What he did not think about, while he was enjoying his shopping spree, was how he'd get all his hardware to the penthouse. At first, he attempted to walk, holding all seven bags in his hands. After about a hundred feet, he gave that up. Nick went back into the store and asked to borrow a shopping cart. The understanding store clerk willingly lent Nick one.

Nick began to walk down the street pushing his cart in front of him. As cars drove alongside him, the drivers would honk their horns or wave, and then pass him. Nick couldn't help but think about the *imbecility* of the whole situation—what a strange sight he presented to onlookers. He was a teenager, in a new pinstripe suit, walking a cart of hardware supplies down the main road in town. He almost began to laugh at himself. But it didn't matter. This trip would be worth it.

Imbecility   (im-buh-**sil**-i-tee) – N – feebleness of mind; silliness or absurdity

WORD REVIEW

Dearth	Glut	Levity
Denizen	Imbecility	Pontificate
Diurnal	Indolence	Proprietary
Eminent	Inordinate	Unremitting
Erudition	Inure	

5

Nick *envisioned* what the penthouse would eventually look like after he made improvements: A flower garden in the front yard and a vegetable garden in the back, a brand new white paint job around the outside, all the windows replaced. He would get new carpet and tile—no more rotting wood. And he'd paint each room a different color. The game room would have a huge television set and several recliners. His bedroom would have nothing smaller than a king-size bed.

His dreams carried him until he reached the dirt road toward his new property. The dirt and rocks began to *militate* in battle against his progress with the cart. The front left wheel, which was already jammed in place, fell off, and the cart would have flipped if it weren't for Nick's quick reflex to hold up the left side. Nick went around to the front of the cart and began to pull it forward while keeping the left side balanced.

He pulled and pulled...and pulled. Every step got harder. A pain began to shoot up his left leg and went all the way to his shoulder. The harder it got, the more determined Nick became. After thirty minutes more, he could finally see his property.

Envision	(en-**vizh**-uhn) – V – to picture mentally, generally of the future
Militate	(**mil**-i-teyt) – V – to have effect or influence; to operate against

As he got closer, Nick realized that it may need more work than he had initially thought. It had seemed so perfect beforehand, but now it just looked like a big work-in-progress. The property itself was dangerously overgrown. In some places, the weeds were taller than he was. Even the house itself looked more *dilapidated* than he remembered.

Nick brought his seven bags of supplies into the building. The job seemed so big that he didn't even know where to begin. "I guess the front yard," he decided.

He didn't want to soil his suit, so he went into the bedroom in search of a change of clothes. He always kept a pair of pajamas in the closet for the nights he slept over, so he put them on and pulled up his sleeves. He got out his machete and a few other yard tools, and went outside.

Nick chopped weeds *zealously*; there was passion in his eyes and in his heart that extended to his muscles, working diligently. His speed was incredible. Within an hour, he had almost finished clearing out the front half of the lawn. He continued, only rarely stopping for a quick breather. By about four o'clock, Nick had finished the whole front side. He looked at his job with pride and was pretty optimistic about the whole thing... until he looked at the back half of the property. His heart sank. It was more disheveled than the front! There was no way he could finish the whole yard in one day. He decided to go back into the house and attempt a project a little less terrifying.

Nick reasoned with himself about the best plan of action. He decided to start with the easiest projects and work his way to the harder ones. He began by cleaning the

Dilapidated	(di-**lap**-i-deyt-ed) – ADJ – reduced to or fallen into ruin or decay
Zealously	(**zel**-uhs-lee) – ADV – ardently active, devoted, or diligent

windows. Having just six windows, only one of which was not broken, this was by far the simplest task he could imagine.

After fixing the windows, he had gained enough confidence to try a bigger project, one that he had always wanted to do: paint the house.

He began by placing each individual color in the rooms where they belonged, starting in the game room. Nick got out the rollers and the pan. He opened the *verdant* grass-hued paint, and with his limited, *verdant* knowledge of painting began to roll a zigzag pattern on the wall. Paint flew everywhere. It fell on the floor, made spots on the ceiling, and most of all, covered Nick in green. He *doggedly* covered the walls in paint, going over them numerous times to ensure that every spot was covered.

Finally he was finished. Nick sat down on the floor, wet with spattered green paint, to admire his work. "Pretty good job, Nick," he said to himself. "Pretty good job."

From this point, he was a man inspired. There was not a room in the world that couldn't use the help of Nick and his paint roller. Even though he was merely a *novitiate*, he felt like he could conquer anything.

He went outside and began painting the front of the house. With every splash of paint, the house seemed to be revived with life. The house became like brand new. And as the house got a new coat, so did Nick. Now he was white from head to toe, with only a little green showing underneath.

Next he attempted the library. Burgundy was everywhere, but Nick knew that the contemplative color would

---

Verdant	(**vur**-dnt) – ADJ – 1. of a green color
	2. inexperienced
Doggedly	(**dog**-id-lee) – ADV – persistently
Novitiate	(noh-**vish**-ee-it) – N – beginner in anything; a novice

help him think when he was reading or studying. In this room he even painted the ceiling, or at least the parts of the ceiling that didn't have holes.

His painting speed increased with every room. By the time he got to the bedroom, he was able to finish it within a half hour.

Nick's remodeling project had completely wasted the day away. He had only the kitchen left, but not enough sunlight to finish it. He decided though, that if nothing else, he would at least remove the *threadbare* wallpaper in this last room to prepare for more painting the next day.

As Nick began to pull it off, he realized that he was not actually pulling down wallpaper, but newspaper painted and glued to the wall. *What type of person would be so closefisted that they would paint their own wallpaper rather than buy the real thing?* Nick wondered to himself.

It made him think about the original owner of the property. He and Mrs. Ray had talked about him before, but not even Mrs. Ray knew much. She knew that he had lived a very *monastic* life; he kept mainly to himself and simply farmed most every day. He lived a very quiet life, one without disturbance. Nick thought about it and realized that if he lived by himself, he probably would make wallpaper just to keep himself from being bored.

Nick started from the left and tore the paper down sheet by sheet. It was much harder to take down than regular wallpaper, but he was up to the challenge. The removal process went well. He was just about finished when

Threadbare	(**thred**-bair) – ADJ – meager, scanty, or poor
Closefisted	(**klohs**-fis-tid) – ADJ – stingy
Monastic	(muh-**nas**-tik) – ADJ – pertaining to living a secluded life

he noticed that one small plank in the wall was loose. It had multiple layers of wallpaper on it, so Nick knew that the previous owner must have had trouble with it. Nick wiggled it in order to test its strength, and it fell to the floor. *I've had this house for one day, and I'm already breaking it,* he thought.

Nick was curious to discover the type of insulation his penthouse had, so he looked inside the hole. It looked like more newspaper. *At least it's not asbestos,* he thought. He reached inside to grab some. When he pulled it out, his hand was filled with money.

WORD REVIEW

Closefisted	Militate	Verdant
Dilapidated	Monastic	Zealously
Doggedly	Novitiate	
Envision	Threadbare	

6

His eyes grew big. His mouth gaped open. His heart was *exultant* and full of joy. All his wildest dreams had suddenly come true.

Nick had a new house, a new suit, a rainbow-colored face and two rainbow-colored hands, and approximately *three hundred thousand* dollars in his backpack. At first he had just sat and stared at it for a full ten minutes. Then he tried counting it out exactly, but there was so much that he kept getting confused. When the shock wore down, he realized it was late and he needed to get home. He practically ran.

Nick fantasized about all the things his *surfeit* of money could buy. That featherweight bike could definitely become a reality. He could buy clothes, sunglasses, video games, and furniture for his house. He didn't have to stop there. He could start a company, rent an office building—the possibilities were endless. He could even buy a Ferrari!

As he daydreamed about ways to spend his money, he passed by Eugenia Ray's house. He saw her sitting on her porch fanning herself. She waved at him and he waved back. Seeing her opened his mind to a whole new world of possibil-

---

Exultant	(ig-**zuhl**-tnt) – ADJ – highly elated; triumphant
Surfeit	(**sur**-fit) – N – excess

ities. He could give some of his money to those who needed it. He could buy Mrs. Ray an air conditioning system.

It would be so amazing to help someone who had always been there for him. At that moment, Nick decided with certainty that he would not be *parsimonious* with this money and started thinking about how he would share it. It was a gift to him, and it would only be right for him to continue the cycle.

He thought about his mom and what she would like as a present. Nick knew that she had saved money for a long time in order to buy his new suit, so he wanted to give her something great. This gave him an idea. He took a detour on the way home to the Sunrise Spa and Resort. His mom spent all day making sure other people were comfortable. It was time for her to be waited on and pampered.

The clerk stifled a laugh as he walked into the resort reception. Nick's green, blue and burgundy face was quite comical, especially paired with his brand new suit.

"Welcome to Sunrise," she said. "How may I help you?"

"Hi, I'm looking to buy a full day spa treatment."

"Well sir, we have a full day package that includes a deep muscle massage, mineral bath, rejuvenating skin treatment for your face, nutrient body wrap, and our *salubrious,* rejuvenating mud soak. However, sir, you will not be allowed to take part in our services until after you have received a bath. Sunrise has an image of cleanliness and professionalism. Our clients do not want to find chunks of paint in their mineral bath and *emollient* lotions. Is that

---

Parsimonious	(pahr-suh-**moh**-nee-uhs) – ADJ – sparing or frugal
Salubrious	(suh-**loo**-bree-uhs) – ADJ – favorable to health
Emollient	(i-**mol**-yuhnt) – ADJ – having the power of softening or relaxing

clear?" she asked, **askance.**

"I'm here to buy a package for my mom," replied Nick defensively.

The receptionist's **demeanor** completely changed from forbidding to friendly. Her grimace turned into a big, welcoming smile. "Oh. Well, in that case," she said, "a full day's package will cost two hundred and ninety-five dollars. Cash or credit?"

Nick pulled out a glut of cash and counted out the money.

"What's your mom's name?"

"Sarah Franklin."

The receptionist smiled and wrote the name in elegant cursive on a gift certificate. She handed it to him and ended the meeting with, "Thank you. Have a great day!"

To top off his gift, Nick headed for the local florist. His mom loved flowers, but never had the time or money to get them. Ever since she was a little girl she'd loved orchids. Her wedding bouquet had even been made of them. Nick ordered the nicest arrangement of orchids that he could find. He became really excited about his mom's gift—surprisingly, the most excited he had been on this very exciting day.

When Nick got home, he couldn't wait to see his mom. She was still at work when he arrived, so he immediately changed clothes and took a shower. Then he sat in his house and waited. He turned on the television, but he was way too energized to pay any attention to it. He kept standing up and walking around the room,

---

Askance	(uh-**skans**) – ADV – with suspicion, mistrust, or disapproval
Demeanor	(di-**mee**-ner) – N – conduct; behavior

randomly laughing out loud at the thought of the day's luck.

His mom was already smiling when she walked through the door. "Honey, I brought your favorite, Panda King! Tonight is a night to celebrate," she said. When she looked at him, she knew something was up. "Are these for me?" she asked when she saw the orchids. Then her excitement turned to concern. "Did you spend your bicycle money again? Now, I do *not* want you to grow up to be a *wastrel*; you need to learn to save."

Nick realized at this moment that he couldn't tell his mom about the money until after he had spent it. She'd make him put it all in a savings account for college. He would let her know after he had bought his Ferrari.

"Mom, I know I couldn't have done half as well in court today without that suit. I wanted to give you this in return." Nick handed his mother the certificate for the spa package. She looked at its gold-printed ink and the inscription with her name. Sarah Franklin was not a *lachrymose* person, but this kind gesture brought tears to her eyes.

"You are a very foolish boy," she said softly. "And if I weren't such a selfish person, I couldn't accept such a generous gift...I love you, Nick."

As his mom gave him a giant hug, Nick decided that he liked giving away money. And he had quite a bit that he could donate without even touching his Ferrari fund!

"Come on, honey. Let's eat our dinner," said Mrs. Franklin as she pulled herself away from her son. They sat down at their dinner table and enjoyed their Chinese feast.

Wastrel	(**wey**-struhl) – N – a wasteful person; spend-thrift
Lachrymose	(**lak**-ruh-mohs) – ADJ – given to shedding tears

Afterward, during their nightly television viewing, Nick asked his mom a question. "How much does the church need to reopen the community center?"

"Well, there's really no hope of that happening, sweetheart," she responded. "I know they've tried to raise the money for over a year. It's something ridiculous, like a hundred thousand dollars."

Nick *feigned* disappointment, but inside he was happy. He knew where his excess money would go: to the church. For the rest of the night he thought about all the people who would be helped by the reopening of the community center. When he went to bed, his heart was full.

What an incredible day!

Feign   (feyn) – V – to pretend; to represent fictitiously

WORD REVIEW

Askance

Demeanor

Emollient

Exultant

Feign

Lachrymose

Parsimonious

Wastrel

Salubrious

Surfeit

7

Nick woke up early the next morning. He jumped out of bed, got dressed, and made another early trip to the office of Mr. Bering. The door was open when he arrived, and it appeared as though Mr. Bering was in the midst of cleaning. There was a mop and bucket on the floor, the desk was cleared off, and the windows were opened to air out the chemicals. Mr. Bering came in behind him.

"Nick, I wasn't expecting you," he said. "You're still rejoicing over our verdict, I see." Nick's cheerful demeanor was evident. "What brings you to my humble—and freshly cleaned—office today?"

"I need you to represent me again...and since you're my lawyer, you're not allowed to share my information with anyone, right?"

"Already in legal trouble, eh?" Bering responded, concerned. "Well as your lawyer, what you say to me is strictly confidential. We need to shut these windows before you say more."

Nick began shutting the windows, while Mr. Bering closed the door. Then they sat down. "Spill," Mr. Bering commanded.

"I found $300,000 in my house." Nick paused for a moment for Mr. Bering to absorb that. "First of all," he went on, "I want to know if it's mine or if I have to give it to the police or something. Secondly, if it is mine, I want to donate $100,000 to the Second Bloomington Church

Community Center, and I need you to deliver the money from me anonymously."

"Wow," Bering whispered, stunned. He was silent for a moment, and then shook his head in wonder. "Are you kidding? I know you're normally a *veracious* kid, but this is unbelievable!"

"Oh, I promise I'm not making this up," Nick said.

"No, I believe you, it's just…I've never heard of such a thing!" He shook his head again and smiled. "Well, your deed to the property includes real property and personal property on the land, so that money belongs to you. And having me act as a *liaison* between you and the church is a great idea. If people knew you had that kind of money, it would attract a whole lot of unwanted attention. Your secret is safe with me, of course…I just can't believe this! So much money for the church? It's such a *meritorious* gift!"

"I just know that so many people can be helped by it," Nick said. It was important that Mr. Bering understand his heart. "With needs for the gym for the kids and the air conditioning for the elderly, it's a shame that nobody has helped sooner."

"Well, have you thought about what you're going to do about the rest of it? You could buy a *profusion* of toys or gizmos with this much money."

Veracious	(vuh-**rey**-shuhs) – ADJ – habitually speaking the truth; truthful; honest
Liaison	(lee-ey-**zawn**) – N – a person who initiates and maintains a contact or connection between two parties
Meritorious	(mer-i-**tawr**-ee-uhs) – ADJ – deserving praise, reward, esteem, etc.
Profusion	(pruh-**fyoo**-zhuhn) – N – abundance; a great quantity or amount

"Honestly," Nick answered, "I need a car, and I've always wanted a Ferrari. I don't need a new one or anything. I'm just tired of walking around all the time."

"A Ferrari is a big jump from walking around on foot."

"Well, I figure that if I can get some new clothes and an awesome car, I will have an easier time at school fitting in."

"That Ferrari is going to have to be your last expenditure, because if you go around town in one of those, people are going to know that something is up. I suggest that you keep walking around until you figure out exactly what you want to do with the rest of your money. Now, I have a safe here in the office, and if it's OK with you, I'd like to keep your money here in the box. I would feel a lot more secure about it." Nick nodded. "Here, let me get you a contract."

Mr. Bering searched through his files for a contract that would apply to their situation—though he certainly had never been in a situation like *this* before! He pulled out the basic agent/client paperwork, and then began marking through the contracts, adding and removing phrases. When he was finished, he placed several sheets of paper in front of Nick.

"Read these, please, and sign them on the bottom," said Bering.

Nick *perused* the contract carefully. It was a basic agreement that said that Nick was going to allow Mr. Bering to keep his money and distribute it as Nick directed—nothing more than formally putting into words what they had already decided. Nick trusted that Mr. Bering would

---

Peruse (puh-**rooz**) – V – read through, as with thoroughness or care not *exploit* his position of authority and take advantage of Nick's inexperience. He signed all the papers necessary. Mr. Bering went to the other room and made several copies. He gave the original contract to Nick.

"OK, that's it. Now I can't steal your money—not that I ever would, of course. It's all in writing. I'll keep your money here until it's all used up or until otherwise directed by you."

"Thanks Mr. Bering, you're awesome," Nick responded. He left the office with a grin on his face.

Exploit   (**ek**-sploy-t) – V – to use selfishly for one's own ends

WORD REVIEW

Exploit	Meritorious	Profusion
Liaison	Peruse	Veracious

8

A *throng* of people was standing around the Liberty book stand, all of whom had newspapers in their hands. The *vociferous* sound of chatting voices filled the area. Such a great commotion attracted the interest of Celeste Bering, who was on her way to the Hamburger Hut. "Anonymous Donor Rescues Community Center," read the front page headline. Celeste picked up the latest copy of Bloomington Times and began to peruse it.

> "A cash donation of $100,000 was received yesterday evening by the congregation of Second Bloomington Church in order to reopen their community center. Reverend William Grey expressed immense gratitude to the individual who made his community center possible for another year. When asked what he would do if he met the donor, he joyfully said, 'I would have my wife prepare whoever it is a feast in our home!' The cash sum was delivered by Mr. James Bering. 'I merely act as an *emissary* for a client who wants to see the people of Bloomington blessed by the

Throng	(throng) – N – a crowd
Vociferous	(voh-**sif**-er-uhs) – ADJ – crying out loudly; clamorous
Emissary	(**em**-uh-ser-ee) – N – an agent sent on a mission or errand

use of this facility,' Bering said. He declined to answer any questions about the identity of the donor. The cash has been deemed untraceable."

This incredible story *piqued* the journalistic interest of Celeste. Normal front-page news in Bloomington involved a cat being rescued from a tree or a local politician holding an event. This was the biggest news on the front page of Bloomington Times since the blizzard that happened in 1988. If Celeste could be the first reporter to scoop the identity of this wealthy individual, she would certainly make front-page news.

Celeste took her copy of the newspaper and rushed toward Hamburger Hut. Her mind was rapidly firing questions about the possible suspects.

There were only three people in the entire town with enough money to qualify as possibilities. The first was Mayor Hill, who always seemed to have enough resources to out-campaign anyone who tried to oppose him in the mayoral election. Secondly, there was the *reclusive* Mrs. Peabody, who lived alone on the largest estate in Clarksville County. People called her "Old Lady Crotchety" because of her continuously *bilious* behavior. Then, of course, there was Jack Ponder. He was the youngest of the three, unmarried and probably in his thirties. He had worked on Wall Street until just a few years ago. Nobody knew how much money he had, but they knew it was a lot. People said that he settled down in Bloomington because he was hiding from the police. They figured that

Pique	(peek) – V – to affect with a lively curiosity; to excite
Reclusive	(ri-**kloos**-iv) – ADJ – living in seclusion; apart from society
Bilious	(**bil**-yuhs) – ADJ – peevish; testy; cross

he probably stole most of his money from the company or clients who employed him.

Celeste had quite a bit of investigating to do.

Lunchtime at the Hamburger Hut was enjoyed almost entirely by teens. Its owner, Santiago Garcia, offered a two-for-one lunchtime special for everyone under eighteen in order to attract the high school crowd.

Celeste arrived fifteen minutes late for her regular appointment. Already waiting at the usual table were the girls who formed her exclusive *clique*: Misty Vaughn, Tracie Winger, and her best friend Sandra Eddleston. The four girls had unofficially reserved that particular table every Tuesday, Thursday, and Saturday.

"Where have you been?" asked Sandra, concerned.

"Ladies, the news stops for no man—or woman, for that matter," she responded.

"We went ahead and ordered you the Mushroom Swiss," Misty said.

"'Cause you know we weren't waiting," added Tracie. "What story's so big that you would place *it* before *us*? You'd better say it's not a cat in a tree."

Celeste paused and looked around dramatically. "I present to you the mystery of the summer," she said as she placed the paper in the middle of the table. "I am going to scoop this story, and you are all going to be jealous of my fame."

"Oh, this *is* interesting," Sandra responded. "But it doesn't seem that hard. All you have to do is ask your dad."

"Do you honestly think my dad would tell me? He takes the whole attorney/client privilege thing way too seriously."

Clique   (klik) – N – a group that is snobbishly exclusive

"Well I'm pretty sure it's Old Lady Crotchety," said Misty. "Ryan told me that the closer she gets to death, the more generous she becomes. His dad did some plumbing work for her a few weeks ago, and he got paid in jewelry. It was a pretty *opulent* gift for someone so stingy."

"At this point in time, Mrs. Peabody is my *cardinal* suspect, but I do have a few other possibilities."

Their burgers arrived then, ending the conversation. They all began to eat, or at least attempt to eat, their meals. None of the girls could ever finish their food, and it was always the custom of Ryan and his best friend Larry to come several minutes after lunch and eat their leftovers. Not to break the tradition, they both showed up a few minutes later.

"How's it going, ladies?" Ryan asked in a cocky manner.

"Fancy seeing you two here," Tracie responded, unsurprised.

"Haha. You are too cute," Larry laughed.

"I love it when you girls eat here," Ryan said as he kissed Misty on the cheek.

"I even got mayonnaise on mine for you," Misty said.

"You are a real doll. I love you so much." Ryan got on his knees and jokingly said, "Misty Elizabeth Vaughn, will you marry me?"

"Oh, I'm so surprised," she responded dryly. "I don't know what to say."

"Just give me your hamburger as a sign of your eternal love and devotion."

Opulent	(**op**-yuh-luhnt) – ADJ – richly supplied; abundant or plentiful
Cardinal	(**kahr**-dn-l) – ADJ – of prime importance; primary

Celeste found their entire sentimental conversation to be disgustingly *saccharine*. She knew that the only reason Misty ordered mayonnaise on her burger was to keep Ryan from complaining. He was always mean to her when he didn't get his way.

"I won't let you two get married until you buy her a house," Celeste said.

"Or I could get your dad to help me steal one," he replied.

Celeste grew defensive. "Nick Franklin had legal rights to that property, Ryan. My dad only helped him solidify his claim. You're just upset because you're not smart enough to read the law."

Ryan scowled. "Everyone knows that sometimes laws can be wrong, and maybe you're just too naïve to see it."

Celeste was offended by that statement, because she believed herself to be sophisticated and worldly, anything but an *ingénue*. "Excuse me, gentlemen," she said. "I have some serious reporting to do."

She grabbed the newspaper, hugged and kissed her friends, and walked out of the room. Celeste was irritated by Ryan's behavior. She could *not* tolerate anyone who would *flay* her revered father, especially over something as trivial as a broken-down farmhouse. Sure, the entire situation was a key point of gossip for the townsfolk, but mostly as a humorous happenstance or one of those rare oddities likely to never occur again. Some critics found attorney Bering slightly irrespon-

Saccharine	(**sak**-er-in) – ADJ – of a sugary sweetness
Ingénue	(**an**-zhuh-noo) – N – a naïve and unworldly girl, especially in acting
Flay	(fley) – V – to criticize or reprove with scathing severity

sible for helping a kid gain land, but those were few and far between. Just about the entire town looked on the situation as a comical occurrence.

Celeste moved her mind back to the story she was planning to nail. Her first plan of action was to confront her father about the mysterious donor. Perhaps he would unknowingly give her clues about his or her *clandestine* identity.

When she walked into her house, she saw her dad sitting in the dining room reading the paper. He lowered it on the table and said with a smirk, "It seems as if 'real' reporters can quote your old man. In fact, not only quote, but use him as their star witness. I think maybe you could learn some lessons from this paper." He pretended to still be upset that earlier she had wanted to interview Judge Reinhorn rather than him.

"Ha, ha, ha," she replied, sarcastically. "Extremely funny. Maybe you should do comedy for a living."

"I thought about it, but then I would get too famous. I wouldn't be able to speak to these small-town reporters, and especially not to small-town reporters-in-training."

"What can you tell me about this mysterious donor?"

"So you want an interview? I think you need to learn to stop following the crowd."

"Seriously, Dad, I really want to crack this case. I could totally make the front page with this story."

"I've already said all that I'm going to say," he responded. "I intend to keep my client's information completely secret. It is my lawful duty to do so."

"But, Dad, if you tell me, I could get what I've always dreamed!"

Clandestine   (klan-**des**-tin) – ADJ – secret; private; concealed

"I'm sorry, sweetheart. You're going to have to find out some other way. But if it's any consolation, I believe in you."

Mr. Bering returned the paper in front of his face to hide his grin. The *reparation* he had just received to amend her earlier snub was far too sweet for words. He knew that his silence would not keep Celeste from her front-page article. Her *indefatigable* determination would see to it that she solved the mystery eventually. It was just a matter of perseverance and hard work, lessons he believed she needed to learn anyway.

Celeste marched upstairs to her bedroom with the mystery gnawing at her brain. She needed to interview her three suspects immediately, but she didn't have a car. Celeste did what she always did and called Sandra.

"Hey, Sandra," she said when her friend picked up.

"Oh, hey, Celeste. Long time, no see," Sandra replied.

"What are you doing this afternoon?"

"Nothing much, why?"

"Would you mind driving me to Mrs. Peabody's estate? I would totally be indebted to you forever."

She could hear Sandra's sigh over the phone. "Celeste, I think when you get your own car, we won't be friends any more. I'll be over in five."

"Thanks, you're the best." Celeste would have to make it up to her later. Right now she had a story to get to the bottom of.

She hung up the phone. Celeste never wasted time

Reparation   (rep-uh-**rey**-shuhn) – N – the making of amends for wrong or injury done

Indefatigable   (in-di-**fat**-i-guh-buhl) – ADJ – incapable of being tired out; not yielding to fatigue

with meaningless *palaver* in phone conversations. She was annoyed by those who took ten minutes to say one thing. So her calls were usually brief and to the point.

Sandra pulled up in front of Celeste's house and honked. Celeste grabbed her notebook and pen and headed out to the car. The road to Mrs. Peabody's estate was very pleasant with blossoming trees, quaint cottages, and a few frolicking horses in the fields. The Peabody Manor itself was elegantly old. As they pulled up under the carport, Celeste admired the intricate wood relief patterns on the ceiling, walls, and continued on the front door. It all appeared so elegant and *urbane*.

Celeste and Sandra got out of the car and walked to the front door. Celeste knocked hard on the solid wooden board. Within moments, they could hear feet scurrying across the floor. The door was quickly cracked open.

"Who is it?" requested a friendly voice.

"I'm Celeste Bering, and this is Sandra Eddleston. We're here to see Mrs. Peabody."

The maid opened the door to the two girls. "Come on in," she replied. "If you'll give me just a moment, she'll be right out." The *amenable* maid politely excused herself down the hall.

A very irritated voice could be heard coming from the other side of the corridor. "I guess that's Old Lady Crotchety," joked Sandra quietly. Celeste shushed her when she saw a wheelchair being rolled in the distance.

"What brings you two to my humble home?" said the old woman abruptly as she was wheeled into the room.

Palaver	(puh-**lav**-er) – N – profuse and idle talk
Urbane	(ur-**beyn**) – ADJ – suave; elegant or refined
Amenable	(uh-**men**-uh-buhl) – ADJ – disposed or ready to yield or submit perception

"Well ma'am," responded Celeste, intimidated, "I came to investigate an anonymous donation given to Second Bloomington Church."

"Well, then what is your friend doing here, besides looking stupid?" Even though she appeared to be ailing in health, Mrs. Peabody's mind was still *acute.*

"I drove her here," replied Sandra.

"She speaks and she drives. How wonderful." Sarcasm oozed from her lips. Sandra was shocked by the *impudence* of the old lady, because in her mind elderly people were universally friendly and docile.

"We've heard," interrupted Celeste, "that you have been given to a little bit of generosity lately. Jewelry in exchange for plumbing work, for instance."

"Look around my home for a bit," said Mrs. Peabody.

Celeste looked around the room. There was a complete dearth of furniture and decorations. It was very tidy, just…empty.

"If you think," Mrs. Peabody said, "that I've been given to generosity lately because I want to make some friends before I die, you are very wrong. I have lived my whole life without them; I do not need them now. And to think that I would give away my money simply to have people sing mournful *dirges* at my funeral—ridiculous!"

"Why the generosity then?" asked Celeste.

"Are you blind? I'm flat broke! Jewelry is the only thing I have of value any more. My great house is rather a

Acute	(uh-**kyoot**) – ADJ – sharp or penetrating in intellect, insight, or perception	
Impudence	(**im**-pyuh-duhns) – N – bold insolence	
Dirge	(durj) – N – song or hymn of grief or lamentation	

deceitful illusion—only a *vestige* of my former opulence. The only thing I have left is Katherine here," she said while pointing to the maid. "And I know she only sticks around because I willed her the estate."

"Oh, I am so sorry, Mrs. Peabody," apologized Celeste. "I didn't mean to…uhh…I won't tell anybody."

"Don't worry about it. Tell everyone you see! I don't care what people think about me. I was not blessed with *bonhomie*, and a reputation for unfriendliness is something that I have lived with for a long time."

"Well, thank you for your time," Celeste said. The two girls shook Mrs. Peabody's enfeebled hand and walked out the door. They both got in the car, but Sandra didn't start it. She paused for a moment, and then turned to Celeste.

"You know, Celeste, I don't come on these trips to get made fun of," she said.

"Mrs. Peabody was just playing. It was just a joke," Celeste replied defensively.

"No, it was not a joke, and you did *not* stand up for me."

"She was just…"

"No! If you won't stand up for me in front of a helpless, cranky old woman, when *will* you stand up for me? I'm your best friend! Or at least, I have a car."

"Sandra, I'm sorry. That will never happen again."

"Where would you like to go, miss?" Sandra responded sarcastically.

Celeste sighed. "I need to go to City Hall. The mayor's my next suspect." She paused. "Sandra, I really am sorry." She hoped things were OK between them.

Vestige	(**ves**-tij) – N – a trace, mark, or visible sign left by something
Bonhomie	(**bon**-uh-mee) – N – good-natured, easy friendliness

"I'm going to drop you off at City Hall. You can walk home. It's close."

Definitely not OK.

Sandra started the car and drove out of Mrs. Peabody's carport. She would not turn her head to look at Celeste. *Ruminating* on how to resolve the argument, Celeste kept her distance and her silence. The quiet continued until they reached downtown. The car stopped in front of the city hall. "I'm going to the beauty parlor," Sandra said. "I just remembered an appointment that I scheduled for exactly right now." Celeste could hear the anger in her voice. She got out of the car and it sped away. The mayor had promised steady office hours in his last election campaign—"Nine to five every weekday," he'd said. His absence from the office was his opponent's main criticism of him. Although Mayor Hill initially had good intentions, it was known by the entire town that after a few months he kept this energetic schedule only *languidly*. Celeste hoped that on this day he would be there.

She walked into the mayor's office. His secretary, Ms. Greenwald, was typing at her desk. She looked up and smiled at Celeste.

"Hi, Celeste, what brings you to the office today?"

"Oh, the usual, an investigation. Is the mayor in?"

"Nope, not right now, and he won't be coming back in for the rest of the day."

"Is there any way you could call him?" Celeste asked.

"Well, I'm really busy right now, but for you… I guess." Ms. Greenwald picked up the phone and dialed it.

Ruminate	(**roo**-muh-neyt) – V – to go over in the mind repeatedly and often casually or slowly
Languidly	(**lang**-gwid-lee) – ADV – sluggishly in character or disposition

She held the receiver to her ear for a few seconds. Then she hung up.

"Looks like he's not answering. I wonder what he could be doing that is too important for my call? No matter. Sorry about this, Celeste."

Ms. Greenwald resumed typing. Celeste paused in the office, and then interrupted her. "Ms. Greenwald, I see how busy you are and I don't mean to *perturb* you, but do you know the soonest I could reach the mayor?"

Ms. Greenwald looked up from her desk, "There's a City Council meeting tonight at eight o'clock. He'll be there."

"Thank you. I really appreciate it." Celeste left the office and headed for the beauty salon, which was in close *propinquity* to her current location. She knew that she needed to settle her argument with Sandra as soon as possible. The short walk to the parlor allowed Celeste some time to think. With every step she took, she felt more and more remorse.

As she approached the beauty salon, she could hear the mindless *prattle* coming from inside the building. As in any other small town, the beauty parlor was the hub of gossip. The room was filled with women, and when Celeste entered, their voices seemed to get louder. She saw Sandra in the back getting a shampoo.

Celeste walked toward her, and with every chair she passed, she caught a new snippet of gossip.

—"Did you hear what Mrs. Tamar wore to church?"—
—"I know!"—

—"And what a nice new car he bought for his grandchild. He will be so spoiled!"—

Perturb	(per-**turb**) – V – to disturb greatly in mind
Propinquity	(proh-**ping**-kwi-tee) – N – nearness in place or time
Prattle	(**prat**-l) – N – trifling or empty talk

—"That's at least what Becky told me. I never believe. . ."—

—"I don't know where the mayor got the money, but I hear he's been meeting with an out-of-town businessman."—

This last snippet of information caught Celeste's attention; however, she had a more pressing need to find Sandra, so she didn't ask any questions. Sandra was relaxing in the chair when Celeste reached her.

"Sandra, I'm sorry for letting Old Lady Crotchety *deride* you and not sticking up for you," Celeste said. Sandra did not acknowledge her voice. The sound of the water on Sandra's head mixed with the sound of gossiping voices kept Sandra from hearing her.

"Sandra," Celeste said louder, "I promise it will never happen again. Please, can we be friends?"

There was still no reply.

Celeste began to shout. "I'm a bad friend and a bad person, and I haven't felt this bad since I stuck gum in Mary Beth's hair in third grade."

Suddenly, the entire room went silent. Celeste's face turned red. Sandra lifted her head and said, "Well, I guess that's payback enough."

"Could you hear me the whole time?" Celeste asked, incredulous.

"Yes, but it was fun."

"What can I do to make it up to you?"

"You are going to take me to the movies tonight. Buy me popcorn, a soda, and some candy."

Deride (di-**rahyd**) – V – to subject to bitter or contemptuous ridicule

"Tonight's not good," interjected Celeste. "There's a City Council meeting, and I need to interview the mayor."

"What is with your extreme interest in this case? You're not trying to solve a crime! You're trying to uncover some *philanthropic* donor, who doesn't even wish to be revealed. Your whole purpose in writing this story is total self-centered, *egocentric* pride!" She looked Celeste in the eye. "You need to decide between me and this news story."

"You are completely right," responded Celeste. "I don't know what has gotten into me. I want to take you to the movies tonight and buy you all that stuff."

"Oh, you're too kind," Sandra replied exaggeratedly. "I can see that you truly value our friendship. Now I have got to get my hair done before our date tonight. You run along home and I'll pick you up at seven."

"OK, you're the boss," Celeste said. She told Sandra good-bye and left the building. Celeste thought about her motivation as she walked home. She had always wanted to be a reporter, but she never realized that trying to get there could hurt the people she loved. At that moment she *avowed* never to let her reporting get in the way of her relationships again. She would no longer ask her dad to betray his client's trust, even if it meant losing a front-page story. She would stop dragging Sandra along solely for the use of her car. And, most importantly, she would try to make the news she reported

Philanthropic	(fil-uhn-**throp**-ik) – ADJ – benevolent; dispensing aid from funds set aside for humanitarian purposes
Egocentric	(ee-goh-**sen**-trik) – ADJ – limited in outlook or concern to one's own activities or needs
Avow	(uh-**vou**) – V – to declare assuredly

something valuable. No more writing rag sheet stories. No more gossip news. *From now on, I'm letting ethics guide my pen,* she thought to herself. *Well, at least until another big story breaks.*

WORD REVIEW

Acute
Amenable
Avow
Bilious
Bonhomie
Cardinal
Clandestine
Clique
Deride
Dirge
Egocentric

Emissary
Flay
Impudence
Indefatigable
Ingénue
Languidly
Opulent
Palaver
Perturb
Philanthropic
Pique

Prattle
Propinquity
Reclusive
Reparation
Ruminate
Saccharine
Throng
Urbane
Vociferous
Vestige

9

"What a blessed, blessed person I am!" Mrs. Ray *extolled* her new air conditioning system. She and Nick sat in her living room drinking tea. "In the heat of the day like this, I couldn't even walk into this room! Now look at us, sitting and drinking some ice-cold tea. I couldn't be cooler if I tried!"

Nick gazed around the room. The portraits on the wall had collected large amounts of dust. The piano looked as if it had not been touched in years. The coffee table didn't even have rings or scratches. Everything appeared to be unused.

"Now I can come in here," she continued, "and enjoy being indoors, away from mosquitoes and the sun. I just wish I could know who did this for me. I want to do something nice in return."

Nick could see that Mrs. Ray was frustrated being so *benighted* about the identity of her mysterious air conditioning donor, so he attempted to comfort her. "I'm sure whoever it was would want you to just enjoy it without worrying," he said.

"I'm sure you're right," she answered. "It *is* a gift. Thanks, dearie."

It made Nick feel so good to see Mrs. Ray relish

| *Extol* | (ik-**stohl**) – V – to praise highly |
| *Benighted* | (bi-**nahy**-tid) – ADJ – existing in a state of intellectual darkness |

her new air conditioner which was an effective *palliative* of the oppressive heat. And the difference the unit made was unbelievable—much better than her old hand fan. He was just happy to give something back to the woman who had been so nice to him for so many years. He wanted to spend more time with her, but today Nick had a mission: to search for needs in the community and fill them.

"Thanks for the tea, Mrs. Ray, but I really need to be going."

"Leaving so quickly?" She sighed and then smiled. "Well, I know you kids have so many things to do these days. Thanks for stopping by. Come back any time!"

Nick walked down the street and tried to calculate his total costs so far. He figured that it would cost around $130,000 to buy himself his new car and some new clothes, and he had already given away $100,000 for the community center and $5,000 for Mrs. Ray's air conditioning. That left him with about $65,000 to give away. He knew that the suffering city was *replete* with need. He just had to find it.

As Nick walked down the street, he examined the houses he passed. Some needed painting…but he couldn't paint everyone's house, and it seemed like a minor, *niggling* need anyway. He wanted to give his money to people who *really* needed it. As he continued walking, the houses kept getting bigger, and the bigger they got, the more discouraged he became. Perhaps this was not the best way to find need in his city.

He was distracted from his thoughts when he saw Bob, the town postman. Bob had been the town's only

Palliative	(**pal**-ee-ey-tiv) – N – something that moderates intensity
Replete	(ri-**pleet**) – ADJ – abundantly supplied; full
Niggling	(**nig**-ling) – ADJ – petty; bothersome or persistent

mail carrier for as long as Nick could remember. He was a friendly guy, and everyone loved him. He even befriended Old Lady Crotchety, being the only person ever invited to come to her manor on Christmas Eve. Nick **accosted** Bob on the sidewalk, hoping to get some help with his mission.

"Hey, Nick, how's it going?"

"Pretty good. I have a lot to be thankful for," Nick responded.

"I think you got your house deed in the mail today. There was a real important-looking envelope addressed to you from the courthouse. That's a pretty sweet deal, huh?"

"Yeah, it's been greater than I could have imagined."

"Well I'm glad you're taking care of that old property now. My house is right around there, and you've turned that eyesore into something a lot more respectable. I'm sure my property value is soaring through the roof!"

"Thanks," Nick said. "I do what I can." He looked around and noticed Bob didn't have a car. "Are you walking home?"

"My junkie car broke down again. I keep trying to get it fixed, but to no avail…Anyway, I've got to get going. I have a lot of ground to cover."

After they waved good-bye and parted ways, Nick began to smile. He had found his next gift recipient. Buying a new car for Bob would be awesome. Nick knew that Bob was putting four kids through school, and he would never make such a large expenditure on himself. It was a legitimate need, and Nick was excited to have found one. But he wasn't going to stop here. He had much more

---

Accost   (uh-**kos**-t) – V – to approach and speak to, often purposefully

searching to do.

The sun was *insufferably* hot that day. Nick could feel it beating down his neck. His forehead was covered with sweat. He couldn't help but dream of his Ferrari. In those wheels, traveling through town would not be a chore. He could go from one spot to the next without having to brave the weather.

This thought motivated him even more to find recipients for his gifts. As soon as he gave away his excess money, he could start buying things for himself.

Nick came to Peabody Field, a gift to the city from Old Lady Crotchety's philanthropic late husband. Nick needed to rest, so he sat on one of the bleachers in the shade. Boys were playing baseball, and he watched. From the first day of summer until the last, the kids of Bloomington *coalesced* at Peabody Field for a season of solid baseball. The regulars came out every day and played all day long.

They were a very entertaining crew to view. Everyone on the field would spit twice a minute and try to play the game between spits. All the kids in the dug out would continuously catcall the players—a loud incoherent sound of screams.

As Nick watched them play, he began to form opinions of the players and of their chances in the major leagues. The pitcher, only ten years old, seemed to be pitching at about sixty miles per hour. He knew that kid had a future. The shortstop also had good odds. He always caught the ball and got it where it needed to go. The first

---

Insufferably	(in-**suhf**-er-uh-buhlee) – ADV – intolerably; unbearably
Coalesce	(koh-uh-**les**) – V – united into a whole

baseman, however, dropped the ball nearly every time it came his way. Even when he caught it in his glove, it would fall out.

Then Nick noticed that his glove was so threadbare that it had a big hole in it. In fact, he noticed that almost all the players had threadbare gloves. Some in the dugout looked like they didn't even have gloves at all. He could not believe that kids who took baseball so seriously would lack such an *integral* piece of equipment for the game. He began to count the kids. He counted twenty-five, but to double check, he called the smallest kid from the dugout. "Hey, come here!"

The little guy, who was probably about eight years old, ran over to the fence where Nick was sitting.

"Yeah? What do you want?" he responded.

"Is everybody here today? All the usual people?"

"Brad's grounded today, but besides him, we're all here."

"Thanks, bud, go back to your game."

The kid shrugged his shoulders and then resumed his catcalls.

Nick also noticed that there was only one bicycle parked outside the field, and even that old and rusting one was not very *estimable*. It was nothing like a Featherweight Mountain Trekker, the bike he knew every kid wanted. *Bicycles could open up a whole new world of fun to these boys*, he thought. Nick could only imagine being ten years old and mysteriously receiving a bike. If it had happened to him, his life would have been absolutely *mirthful*, full of goofing

Integral	(**in**-ti-gruhl) – ADJ – essential to completeness
Estimable	(**es**-tuh-muh-buhl) – ADJ – worthy of esteem
Mirthful	(**murth**-fuhl) – ADJ – full of gladness or gaiety

off and playing around. These thoughts settled him on the idea—new bikes and new gloves for all the baseball kids.

Nick was suddenly distracted by the music of the ice cream truck, a ***dulcet*** sound on such a hot day. The truck pulled up to the field, but of course the baseball boys would not be distracted from their game, so Nick was the lone customer from Peabody Field.

Jerry Fuller, owner of the ice cream truck, was also the owner of a car dealership. Several years ago he had taken an old minivan and refurbished it into Bloomington's only ice cream vender on wheels. On most days, salesmen from the dealership ran the truck around town. They actually had a mandatory number of hours that each person had to fulfill.

Occasionally, when Mr. Fuller became tired of being in the office, he would drive the truck himself. He was a deacon at Second Bloomington Church, so Nick had known him his entire life. As he walked up to the window, Nick was glad to see Mr. Fuller at the helm.

"Hey, Nick! What can I get for you today?" asked Mr. Fuller.

"Can I get the bar shaped like a clown?"

"Sure thing," replied Mr. Fuller as he opened his freezer and pulled one out. Nick began to reach for his wallet when Fuller said, "Don't worry about it. What's an ice cream bar between friends? Is there anything else I can do for you?"

"Thanks for the clown, Mr. Fuller! Actually there might be something you can do…where's your next stop?"

"I'm going straight downtown and then back to my shop," he replied.

Dulcet   (**duhl**-sit) – ADJ – pleasing to the ear

"Is there any way you could give me a ride to downtown?"

"Of course! Just hop right in the back." Mr. Fuller opened the back doors, and Nick climbed inside. Because it was an ice cream truck, there wasn't any room for passenger seating.

"Be careful and hold on tight. I don't want you to get hurt because you're not wearing a seatbelt."

Nick braced himself in the back. The car began the bumpy trip to the center of Bloomington. When the van stopped, Nick thanked Mr. Fuller and got out.

The downtown square had already begun to be *suffused* with decorations in advance of one of the city's major celebrations. The committee for community events was getting a head start this year for their annual Fourth of July extravaganza. The celebration always included carnival food, games, rides, fireworks, and a surfeit of *tawdry* and tacky decorations.

The town bulletin board attracted Nick's attention, so he wandered over to it. Running along its top was a 6-foot red, white, and blue banner, with small United States flags across the bottom. On the board itself were posters made of red, white, and blue construction paper saying, "America Rocks!" and "God Bless America." Posted *contiguous* to the patriotic bulletins there were only two items that were not intended for the Fourth of July. These included several advertisements for Pete's Plumbing, a new discount plumbing shop in the area. "Lower prices, better quality," was its slogan. The other

---

Suffuse	(suh-**fyooz**) – V – to spread over or through
Tawdry	(**taw**-dree) – ADJ – cheap and gaudy in appearance or quality
Contiguous	(kuhn-**tig**-yoo-uhs) – ADJ – near in sequence; touching or sharing a boundary

was a request for a cheap babysitter for Mrs. Roberts. Nick remembered the prayer request Reverend Grey mentioned a few weeks earlier about this situation. Nick did some math in his head. *About sixty days for eight hours for about five bucks an hour equals about . . . two thousand four hundred dollars. I could do that, no problem!*

It was time for Nick to go make his requests with Mr. Bering. Hopefully he could get them worked out by the end of the week. Then Nick could mysteriously receive his Ferrari.

He walked over to the McMillan Building and noticed that the sidewalks were wet with a shallow stream of water, the trail leading through the McMillan Building's front doors. He held tightly to the railing as he went upstairs because the steps appeared extremely slippery. The door to Mr. Bering's office was open, and he watched as Mr. Bering was mopping his floor. Nick knocked on the door.

"Oh, hey, Nick, come right on in," responded Mr. Bering. "One of the pipes broke on the third floor and it's been like an ocean in here until just a few minutes ago. Pete's Plumbing is a lifesaver. Have you thought about how to **apportion** your remaining money among potential benefactors?"

"I know what I want to do," responded Nick. "First, I want to get Bob the postman a new car. His old one doesn't work, and I can't think of a nicer guy to deserve it."

"That would be so nice of you, Nick. I know he could really use one. What type of car?"

"Something nice and dependable. Nothing too fancy."

Apportion (uh-**pohr**-shuhn) – V – to divide and share out
according to a plan

"I could probably get him something really ***commodious*** for between fifteen and twenty thousand that he could use for his job and still be comfortable for the family."

"Perfect," said Nick. "I also want to get Featherweight Mountain Trekkers for all twenty-six boys who play baseball at Peabody Field, along with twenty-six new baseball gloves."

"That's also very generous. I'll have to get those bikes shipped here, and probably the gloves, too, because it's such a large order. I'm going to estimate around eight thousand for all that."

"And I also want to get Mrs. Roberts a babysitter for the entire summer."

"Now I don't know the going rate for babysitters these days. I know it's gone up the last few years, but that should be no more than three thousand." Mr. Bering got out Nick's account book and reviewed his records. "Even if those items run high, you still have about twenty thousand left before even hitting your personal allotted money."

Nick felt the need to ***canvass*** the town again looking for gift recipients. He was tired, so the first need he could find that would cost $20,000 would get it all. Then he could move on.

"Thanks Mr. Bering," Nick said. "As always, I really appreciate your taking care of this for me."

"No problem, buddy. I'm so glad that I'm able to be a part of something as awesome as your anonymous gift giving," Bering replied.

Nick shook his hand, and again went out to find someone in need. His disappointment with having to

---

Commodious   (kuh-**moh**-dee-uhs) – ADJ – comfortable or spacious
Canvass   (**kan**-vuhs) – V – to examine in detail

continue the search was apparent on his face. The whole situation was incredible, but it frustrated him as well, because figuring out whom to give his money to was like an unsolvable *conundrum.* He'd thought that giving away money would be a walk in the park. He never even considered the great responsibility that came with the blessing he had received. *Who knew that being generous and* *altruistic* *would be so difficult?*

Nick walked around downtown for a while, but soon decided to quit. His frustrating task had made him overwhelmingly *dejected* and tired. He went to one of his favorite spots, the Bloomington Library. As in most small towns, the library was also small. There were only two librarians, Mrs. Woodard, the head librarian, and Ms. Rice, who only worked on weekends. Both of them knew Nick by name. Mrs. Woodard was working the front desk when he arrived.

"Nick!" she said, "You haven't been here since school ended! I was beginning to think something had happened to you."

"I've just been really busy lately," Nick responded.

"Well, I'm glad to see you're alive and well," she replied.

Nick walked through the aisles, which he knew like the back of his hand. He had probably read at least one book from every section. He finally hit his favorite spot, the law section. Nick had read every book in this area at least once, yet he never tired of them. He grabbed his

Conundrum	(kuh-**nuhn**-druhm) – N – an intricate and difficult problem
Altruistic	(al-troo-**is**-tik) – ADJ – unselfish with regards to the welfare of others; humanitarian
Dejected	(di-**jek**-tid) – ADJ – cast down in spirits; depressed

favorite, *A Biography of Modern Lawyers*, which he had read so many times that he could probably quote the entire book **verbatim**. It detailed the lives of America's greatest attorneys. Every time Nick read this one, it inspired him to study and work toward achieving his dreams.

Nick sat down on one of the library's couches and began to flip through the pages. He took comfort in the hope this book provided him. Someday, he, too, would be one of the United States' most influential lawyers. He only wished he could read more about them.

Suddenly, Nick realized that $20,000 could buy a new wing of the library. Yes, that would be perfect. One that featured a brand new collection of law books.

Nick smiled, shut his book, and went back to Mr. Bering's office.

Verbatim   (ver-**bey**-tim) – ADV – word for word

WORD REVIEW

Accost	Conundrum	Niggling
Altruistic	Dejected	Palliative
Apportion	Dulcet	Replete
Benighted	Estimable	Suffuse
Canvass	Extol	Tawdry
Coalesce	Insufferably	Verbatim
Commodious	Integral	
Contiguous	Mirthful	

10

"You give the term journalism a *pejorative* connotation because of your untiring ambition," Sandra complained over the phone. "I thought you were over this thing?"

"I was," said Celeste, "but it's not about me any more. There are a lot of people who want to find this guy, assuming it is a guy, and thank him."

"But this goes against your promise to me!"

"I know. That's why I called you first."

Sandra knew that if she didn't give Celeste consent, Celeste would bug her until she received the *accord* to continue the search. "Fine, do what you want. Just count me out this time."

"You're the greatest best friend ever!" Celeste told her.

"I know. I really should get a medal or some other *accolade*."

"Well, I need to get started. I'll talk to you later."

Celeste hung up the phone, excited. She was ready to complete her investigation. Because finding the mayor would be like finding a needle in a haystack, she decided to interview suspect number three: Jack Ponder.

Jack owned an office downtown, yet nobody knew

Pejorative	(pi-**jawr**-uh-tiv) – ADJ – tending to disparage or belittle	
Accord	(uh-kawrd) – N – agreement	
Accolade	(ak-uh-leyd) – N – a mark of acknowledgment	

exactly what he did. Clarence at the phone company said he made several calls during the day to out-of-state places, but other than that the town was clueless as to Ponder's profession. That made him a perfect suspect. Celeste intended to make an unscheduled stop by his office.

She walked downstairs to see her dad sitting in his regular spot at the dining room table, eating lunch.

"When you go back to work, will you drop me off downtown?" she asked.

"Sure, honey, what business do you have down there today?"

"Oh nothing, just going to have some fun."

"Where's Sandra? Why isn't she taking you?" he asked.

Celeste paused.

Bering, aware of his child's often deceptive behavior, grew suspicious.

"What are you going to be doing for fun?" he asked her. "I might want to join you. It's so good being self-employed because I can take a break from my schedule to spend time with my daughter without somebody breathing down my neck."

"I'm going to interview Jack Ponder," Celeste admitted.

"Still trying to figure out this mysterious gift-giving *enigma*, I see."

"Yes. Now will you take me?"

"Of course I will, but I don't want you getting too involved in this. I'm telling you, whoever it is does not want to be found out." Celeste nodded. "Let me finish my lunch, and then we'll head out."

Enigma   (uh-**nig**-muh) – N – something hard to understand or explain

While Celeste waited for her dad to be finished, she *cogitated* over how to approach Mr. Ponder. She couldn't just enter his office and ask him straightforwardly whether or not he had been giving away money. First she had to find out if he even *had* money. Then she needed to figure out his motivation for distributing it. Guilt? Philanthropy? Whatever the reason, she wanted to get to the bottom of it, and with Jack Ponder as a suspect, who knew how good a story she could end up getting?

Celeste and her dad drove downtown. He let her get out right beside Ponder's office.

"Thanks, Dad," she told him.

"No problem."

Celeste walked to the front door and rang the bell. She knew that Ponder didn't have a secretary, so if anyone answered the door, it would be him. And in a few seconds, he did.

"How may I help you?" Ponder asked.

"My name is Celeste Bering and I would like to have an interview with you," she said.

"Me?" he responded, *bemused* by this unexpected visitor. "Why?"

"I'm doing an investigative story about recent town happenings, and I have some questions I'd like to ask you."

"Um. . . OK... Come in."

Mr. Ponder led Celeste into the messy room. His desk was organized, but newspapers were piled all around the room, along with old photographs and random gadgets. Ponder took a seat behind the desk, and Celeste sat in front. She opened her notebook.

Cogitate   (**koj**-i-teyt) – V – to meditate deeply or intently
Bemused   (bi-**myoozd**) – ADJ – confused

"First things first," Celeste said. "What is your profession?"

"I do a little of everything, and a whole lot of nothing. I guess my most concrete job is as a freelance author."

"And before freelancing?"

"I was a sales rep for a Fortune 500… Where are these questions going?"

"Someone's been giving away large gifts anonymously, and there's a chance that the moneys obtained for these presents were *procured* fraudulently. So I came here—"

"—You came here because you suspected me," he finished for her. "Well I'll tell you right now I didn't take any money, and I'm not running away from the law like those old gossips say. The only thing I'm running away from is myself."

"What do you mean?"

"My past life was completely greedy and *hedonistic.* I worked eighty-hour work weeks to get to the top of my profession. I would work all day and spend the rest of my time partying in clubs or bars. That type of life puts a strain on your body, and I had to get help to rescue me from several legal and illegal substances. I was on a high that I thought would never end, until one day I get a phone call from a girl I don't even remember meeting, and she told me she'd had a baby. We did the paternity test and boom, because of my *satyric* lifestyle, I'm a father."

Celeste stifled a gasp. She was so stunned that for once she couldn't think of anything to say.

Procure	(proh-**kyoor**) – V – to obtain by particular care and effort
Hedonistic	(**heed**-n-ist-ik) – ADJ – of the doctrine that pleasure or happiness is the sole or chief good in life
Satyric	(**sey**-ter-ic) – ADJ – lecherous; lascivious

Mr. Ponder continued. "I cleaned myself up fast; *sobriety* hit me like a ton of bricks. I came out here to get away from it all. I've been living off my savings."

"Wow," Celeste said. It was absolutely the last thing she'd expected. "I don't know if the people in our town can handle such a story. It's probably good that you haven't told anybody."

"Life as a hermit is not all it's cracked up to be, Celeste. Sure it's fun for a little while, but it gets lonely. I think there will be a time in the future when James Ponder reenters the world of community and friendship, but for now I still need a little more time to myself."

"Well I'm sure when you *are* ready, the people of Bloomington will be more than willing to welcome you into our city."

"That's what I like about small towns. There is something so righteous and *inviolate* about the hospitality and friendliness. That's what attracted me to Bloomington. That, and the fact that it would allow me the peace to begin my writing career. I had always wanted to become a writer; now I have the opportunity."

"What's with all the papers and junk in here?" Celeste asked.

"For inspiration," Ponder replied. "You'd be surprised at how many stories, and novels, and screenplays are just ripoffs of news headlines or inspired by some old documents."

"If you don't mind my asking, have you written anything yet?"

Sobriety	(suh-**brahy**-i-tee) – N – the quality or state of being sober
Inviolate	(in-**vahy**-uh-lit) – ADJ – not violated or profaned; pure

"Well, I've gotten several short stories published in magazines. Nothing major, but I'm trying to make a name for myself. In fact, I got a call today from my literary agent in New York, saying that a studio might want to option one of my stories for a film. Who knows whether or not that will go anywhere, but maybe."

"Wow, that would be awesome. And what about your child, how's it doing now?"

"It's a girl and her name is Susie. And she's doing fine. I never get to see her because she lives so far away, but she's all right."

"Well, Mr. Ponder, I do apologize for *beleaguering* you for so long with such personal questions. Please forgive my rudeness and my complete lack of respect."

"Don't worry about it. It was my pleasure to be beleaguered."

Celeste excused herself and left the office building. She felt like such a *boor* for practically accusing the innocent Mr. Ponder of fraud. So far, her investigation had only brought her trouble, but with just one suspect left, there was no way she could quit. But how was she going to find the mayor?

Suddenly Celeste noticed the bulletin board filled with decorations. Mayor Hill was required to be at the Fourth of July ceremony! She'd be sure to see him then! Maybe she could see if he'd spill some good information.

Beleaguer	(bi-**lee**-ger) – V – to trouble; to harass
Boor	(boor) – N – a rude or insensitive person

WORD REVIEW

Accolade
Accord
Beleaguer
Bemused
Boor

Cogitate
Enigma
Hedonistic
Inviolate
Pejorative

Procure
Sobriety
Satyric

11

On July Fourth, people began setting up kiosks and booths before dawn. The sound of boiling grease and electric generators filled Peabody Park. Everyone hustled with excitement. All day long local groups would perform before the entire town audience—mostly dance troupes and musical recitals—but the headliner was none other than Joe Harrington, the famous country singer. Fireworks were set to go off as he closed his set with "God Bless America." As always, this year's event was planned to be the *singular* most exceptional town celebration in history. City Hall *heralded* this patriotic sentiment every year, mainly because City Hall always liked to be the *herald* of good news.

Celeste and her folks arrived at about ten o'clock, and the park was already completely filled with people. There was one main line of booths, a section of picnic tables, and the main stage with rows of chairs placed all along the front. Every section was bustling with activity. Celeste immediately asked permission to go check out the attractions.

Singular	(**sing**-gyuh-ler) – ADJ – extraordinary; odd; distinctive
Herald	(**her**-uhld) – V – 1. to signal the approach of something, often with enthusiasm
	2. one that conveys news or proclaims

"That's fine with me," her dad said, "but come find us during the fireworks."

Celeste agreed and left to look for her friends. She made her way through the crowd and headed for the picnic section. If she knew her friends well, they would be sitting there eating—or in their case, not eating—and complaining about the heat. Celeste canvassed the tables, and exactly as she had *augured*, she found the three girls sitting under a big umbrella on the lawn. They were a mismatched set. Misty was wearing a nice summer dress, probably for Ryan's sake, along with some fake pearls. Tracie wore a bathing suit with a tank top and athletic shorts. Sandra had on a big ruffled dress, three layers thick and long-sleeved. It was red, yellow, and black, the colors of the German flag. Her face was wet with sweat. Celeste approached them with a smile.

"What's up, ladies?" she asked *quizzically*.

"You know, enjoying the weather," said Sandra. "Where've you been?"

"I came with my parents; we just got here."

"Why do we come to this thing every year? It's so dull. Next year let's go somewhere else for the Fourth. Maybe the lake or something," said Tracie.

"That's easy for you to say. You don't get to sing with the Guten Tag Choir," responded Sandra with *tepid* excitement bordering on boredom.

"Isn't singing in German on the Fourth of July kind of un-American?" asked Misty.

"It would be, except our performance today is basically classical American songs translated into German,

Augur	(**aw**-ger) – V – to foretell; to foresee
Quizzically	(kwiz-i-kuhlee) – ADV – disbelievingly or curiously
Tepid	(**tep**-id) – ADJ – lacking in passion, force, or zest

like 'Yankee Doodle' and the 'Battle Hymn of the Republic.' As our director says, 'It symbolizes the unification of German citizens with the culture and ideas of the United States.' German was almost America's national language."

"Ladies," Tracie said to change topics, "This year I am going to win the watermelon-eating contest!"

"Tracie," responded Celeste, "you barely eat anything."

"I know," she said. "I've been saving room in my stomach all year. It's at four o'clock, and I expect you all to be there to see me accept my big trophy."

"What time is your performance, Sandra?" Celeste asked.

"Twelve thirty. But don't worry; y'all don't have to come to that."

"Of course we'll be there," Tracie said.

"Well, for now, I'm headed off in search of the *elusive* mayor," Celeste said. "Wish me luck."

"Hey, I think I saw him near the stage earlier," Misty said, "but more likely than not, you'll find him around the food." Her eyes then got big and excited as she saw Ryan in the distance. She stood up and ran into his arms. They began to kiss. Celeste stuck her tongue out at Sandra and made a vomiting sound. Sandra giggled in return.

"You two are just jealous because you don't have boyfriends," commented Tracie.

Truthfully, Celeste's dislike of Ryan **antedated** this recently-established relationship with Misty. Celeste's investigative personality caused her to watch people carefully, and she had been watching Ryan since grade school. To her and her friends, Ryan had always been very kind. His

---

Elusive   (i-**loo**-siv) – ADJ – tending to evade grasp or pursuit
Antedate   (an-ti-**deyt**) – V – to precede; to come before

relationship with Misty had always been relatively respectful. However, Ryan did not value people who were not useful to him. He often bullied weaker people. It was this two-faced *dichotomy* that Celeste found irritating. He could be so nice one minute, and then immediately turn around and be cruel; such *incongruous* behavior was intolerable to her.

"Hey, girls, I'll catch you later," Celeste said as she got up. "I won't forget 12:30 and 4:00."

Celeste wanted to say good-bye to Misty, but she was a little preoccupied, so Celeste just gave her a little pat on the back and walked away.

"'Bye Celeste," Misty called out from behind her.

Celeste wandered through the maze of picnic tables in search of the mayor. There were people everywhere. All the tables were filled, and in between tables several families sat eating on blankets. Celeste had to be cautious with every step she made to ensure that she didn't step on anyone's food or blanket or feet.

She eventually made it to the main drag, right by the stage. Mrs. Reynolds was singing her rendition of "Amazing Grace." Reynolds had once gone to Nashville in search of a music career, but nothing ever came from it. Celeste didn't waste time looking through the back rows of chairs for the mayor. If he was there, he would without a doubt be sitting in the reserved section in the front. Mayor Hill was friendly with everyone, but naturally he took advantage of all *perquisites* and rewards

---

Dichotomy	(dahy-**kot**-uh-mee) – N – something with seemingly contradictory qualities
Incongruous	(in-**kong**-groo-uhs) – ADJ – inconsistent
Perquisites	(**pur**-kwuh-zit) – N – things held or claimed as exclusive rights or possessions, informally shortened to "perks"

that came with his office.

When Celeste made it to the front, she was disappointed to see only her parents. They always sat in the front row with Judge Reinhorn and the City Council members, but currently they were sitting alone. They had already saved Celeste a seat, by her request. She'd had a crush on Joe Harrington ever since she saw him on television, and sitting up front during the concert was just one of the privileged *boons* of being the only daughter of the town's only lawyer.

"Celeste, come here," called her mom. "Sweetie, could you buy your dad and me a funnel cake?" She handed her some money. "If there's any left over, you can keep it."

Her mom handed her a five dollar bill. She took the money and headed toward the main strip of kiosks in search of funnel cakes. Strangely, they were nowhere to be found. She passed all the food booths and headed into the game section, passing ring toss, the gun shoot, and the baseball throw. No funnel cakes in sight. Then she saw a little girl holding one covered in powdered sugar and strawberries.

Celeste stopped the girl. "Where did you get that?" she asked. The little girl pointed farther down the road toward the entrance. Celeste thanked her, and headed in that direction. As she followed the path, Celeste *desisted* from her search when she noticed the dunking booth.

The person sitting behind the target was none other than Mayor Hill.

A huge line of kids waited for their chance to get

Boons   (boons) – N – timely benefits
Desist   (di-**sist**) – V – to cease to proceed or act

him wet. They all must have been terrible shots because Hill was completely dry. Celeste waited in line for her opportunity to interview him. Every time someone threw the ball, she hoped he or she would make the shot. Her anticipation grew as she got closer and closer to the front. Each person continued to miss. When she reached the front of the line, she was all business. "Mayor Hill, can I ask you a few questions?"

"Only if you can get me in this water," he responded.

"Deal." Celeste bought a ball. She threw it and missed terribly. She bought a second one, and her second throw was worse than her first. Her third and fourth tries were closer, but she still didn't hit the mark.

She was about to give up when the mayor called out to her, "Come on! Try it again. It's for charity." Celeste got her last ball. She aimed carefully, drew her hand back, and threw it forward.

The ball hit the target. KERPLUNK! The mayor fell into the pool of water. Celeste walked around to the ladder as Mayor Hill exited, soaking wet.

"What can I do for you?" the mayor asked **glibly**, despite his soaking wet condition.

"There have been some mysterious gifts given to citizens of the town, and I was wondering whether or not you know anything about them," she responded.

"Well, of course I know about them. I'm the mayor! What type of mayor doesn't know the happenings in his own town?"

"What I meant to ask was, do you have any idea of the identity of this mysterious person?"

"What I know," he said, "I can't tell. Actually, I

Glibly   (**glib**-lee) – ADV – marked by ease and informality intend to *promulgate* the information later tonight to the whole town before Joe Harrington takes the stage. But until then, mum's the word."

"Thank you, Mr. Mayor," said Celeste. She shook his wet hand and returned to her search for funnel cakes. This meeting confirmed Celeste's suspicions. She *knew* the mayor was involved. This was just his style. He would do some good things, allow people to talk, and then when everyone in the county was all together, he would announce his involvement. She had to give him credit for the plan's cleverness. It would guarantee him reelection for certain.

More pressing matters took hold of Celeste's mind. She had to buy a funnel cake, *and* find the money to pay for it, now that she'd spent the five dollars at the dunking booth. She again walked toward the entrance, and finally she came upon the funnel cake stand. Ryan and his friend Larry were already in line. Celeste accosted them.

"Hey, Ryan, do you have any spare cash?" she asked.

"A little, what do you need?"

"I need a funnel cake for my mom, but I don't have any money left. Do you think you could spare a couple bucks?"

"OK, but only if I get a favor in return."

"That's fine," said Celeste. "I want one with powdered sugar and apple topping."

Being indebted to Ryan was not Celeste's ideal scenario, but it was much better than going back to her parents empty-handed. When she got the funnel cake, she thanked Ryan and rushed back to the stage. Sandra would

---

Promulgate   (**prom**-uhl-geyt) – V – to make known by open declaration

be performing at any moment, and if Celeste missed it, their friendship would be over for sure. As she wandered in between people, she was *charily* aware of the need to hold the cake carefully. She wanted to be sure it didn't get knocked to the ground by an audience member *jostling* to get closer closer to the stage.

When she arrived to the stage, Sandra had not yet begun her performance. Celeste walked to the front and *purveyed* the cake to her parents, completing the task she had been assigned.

When Mr. Bering spotted the cake, he said dramatically, "Finally I have received a *nostrum* to cure my hunger!"

"Stop being so theatrical, Dad." Celeste replied.

The Guten Tag Choir took the stage then, each member carrying a miniature United States flag. They lined up in a semicircle, and their director took the center position. The sopranos began the opening notes to "The Star Spangled Banner." Celeste watched as Sandra nervously fidgeted on the stage. Sandra disliked being in the public eye, and performing for such a large audience was terrifying to her. Sandra did have a very beautiful voice, though, and Celeste could distinguish it from the others. The choir sang eight songs before taking a final bow. Even though the performance was a little unconventional, the audience applauded and cheered the choir.

Charily	(**chair**-uh-lee) – ADV – cautiously; hesitantly
Jostle	(**jos**-uhl) – V – to make one's way by pushing and shoving
Purvey	(per-**vey**) – V – to supply, usually as a matter of business or service
Nostrum	(**nos**-truhm) – N – a usually questionable remedy, medicine, or scheme

Sandra came out from the back stage several minutes after the performance. She wore a smile on her face and a T-shirt and jeans. She appeared so much more comfortable.

"I'm free!" shouted Sandra. "Now I can relax for the rest of the day."

"You did such a good job," Celeste told her.

"It's all the talent that I have," Sandra joked.

"Whatever," Celeste said. "Hey, I'm ready to have some fun."

"Well, I'm ready to get a snow cone."

Celeste willingly agreed to Sandra's sudden *vagary*, and the two left for the frozen treats. As they walked along the path, Sandra was struck with a *yen* for all the enticing edibles they passed. Before they even made it to the snow cone stand, her hands were filled with food.

"I think I'm so hungry because I was so nervous. You know, when your adrenaline starts going, your body shuts down your digestive system. Getting nervous is a great way to lose weight."

"With all that junk food, I don't think you will have any problem with *emaciation*," Celeste replied.

The line was long when they arrived at the snow cone stand. "Do you even want one of these any more?" asked Celeste.

"Nah, I've got plenty already."

"Well, we've got some time to kill before Tracie's eating contest. What should we do?"

Vagary	(**vey**-guh-ree) – N – an erratic, unpredictable, or extravagant manifestation, action, or notion
Yen	(yen) – N – strong desire or propensity
Emaciation	(i-mey-see-**ey**-shuhn) – N – loss of flesh so as to become very thin

"I know," Sandra said excitedly. "Let's go to the face painting booth! It will be so much fun."

They walked to the booth with the big sign that said "Face Painting." The lady who worked there wore black and had long black hair. She had a very friendly demeanor and welcomed them to her shop.

"Hey, girls, are y'all interested in getting your faces painted?"

"Yup," answered Sandra.

"Well here's a book of possibilities. Look through this and pick something you like."

Celeste and Sandra scrolled through the binder of pictures. They passed flowers, Chinese symbols, and hearts, until they came across the butterflies. Orange and blue, they were so beautiful that they both decided butterflies were the way to go.

"I want the butterfly," Celeste said. "Can we get them on our arms?"

"Of course," the lady in black responded.

Sandra went first. She shivered as the cool paint was sprayed on her arm in the shape of a butterfly. The artist then got out a fine brush and began painting the details of the butterfly. When the girl finished, Sandra was instructed to hold her arm steady and not to touch the figure.

"If I get one, can I pay you back, Sandra?" Celeste asked.

"Sure," she replied.

Sandra sat with Celeste as she underwent the same procedure. It was nearing four o'clock when they finished, so the two girls hustled to get to the pavilion where the watermelon contest was being held. The announcer had already begun speaking when they arrived.

"Today, the ladies of greater Clarksville County and

surrounding areas will *vie* for the top eating prize of the state, the Golden Watermelon. Several of you have trained all year for this competition, and I'm excited to see who takes it. There are just a few rules to go over. First, every bit of watermelon must be eaten by the contestants. No cheating folks! Second, don't steal watermelon from the other competitors. Even if you finish your stack before they do, wait for one of our kind servers to get you some more. This is not a timed contest. We're trying to see who can eat the most watermelon. It doesn't matter how fast you get there. Third, a watermelon slice will only be considered eaten if you get down to the rind. Fourth, if you spit it up, you're out. Ladies, get ready as my lovely assistants bring out the watermelon."

Girls in watermelon-print dresses began to bring out plates of watermelon. Each contestant, about thirty in all, received a plate with ten watermelon slices. Tracie examined her opponents. Most of the women were a lot bigger than she was and probably much more experienced. Instead of intimidating her, though, it *empowered* her. She knew she could beat these ladies at their own game. She did not approach this contest with *diffidence*, but rather confidence.

The announcer called out, "On your mark, get set, GO!!!!"

The women all began chomping on the watermelon slices. Many raced through it, but Tracie had a different strategy. She politely chewed on her pieces, carefully

Vie	(vahy) – V – to strive for superiority
Empower	(em-**pou**-er) – V – to promote the self-actualization or influence of something or someone
Diffidence	(**dif**-i-duhns) – N – the state of being hesitant in acting or speaking through lack of self-confidence

spitting out seeds as she went.

"Slow and steady wins the race!" Sandra called out in encouragement. Tracie acknowledged this shout with a nod and continued eating. Before long, she was on her second plate. She chomped, and chomped, and chomped. Competitors began to drop out. First it was a little girl, then a grandmother. No surprises. A few women left at twenty-one, then a few more at twenty-five. The number of ladies diminished with every slice. Tracie was a little behind the pack, but slowly she caught back up with them. Twenty-five slices, thirty slices, forty slices—her determination was stronger than iron. When the competition reached fifty slices, it was down to five people: Mary Fink, last year's grand champion, a lady very **conversant** with eating competitions; Sara Stanley, the head cook of Stanley's Steak House; Betty Adams, an average-looking soccer mom; Trudy Jones, the most competitive woman in Clarksville County who had won just about every other local competition except this one; and Tracie. It seemed as if they were all in it for the long haul.

At slice fifty-five the competition changed. The announcer brought all the finalists together and sat them in a row. From this point on, they would all be given one slice at a time. Fifty-six—everyone stayed in it. Fifty-eight—all survived. Fifty-nine—this was the last round for Betty Adams; she could not finish her slice. Sixty-one—four competitors lasting. Sixty-three—as Sara Stanley took her last bites of watermelon, the whole lot came back up. She was disqualified.

With only three competitors left, the game got

Conversant   (**kon**-ver-suhnt) – ADJ – having knowledge or experience

serious. It was exactly as Tracie had pictured. All three were going to eat until victory or death. Mary Fink, with her round *porcine* figure, still looked hungry. Trudy's eyes were filled with *cupidity* for the longed-for Golden Watermelon.

Tracie knew that she could not last much longer. Her *burgeoning* stomach could only grow so big! But she would never show it to her competition. She continued to scowl with the attitude of a winner.

Sixty-four went very slowly for Tracie. Every bite seemed laborious. Her digestive system was tired of the mushy pink fruit she was placing inside it.

Tracie was working on sixty-five when Mary Fink began to choke on a small piece. She started coughing and eventually had to spit it up.

Trudy Jones stood up in her seat and shouted, "You're disqualified!"

Surprised by this outburst, Mary Fink looked to the announcer.

"I'm sorry, Mary, but the rules state that any form of regurgitation disqualifies a contestant. Maybe next year," he said.

Mary looked devastated. It was clear that she had plenty more room for watermelon in her belly.

The *egregious* display of poor sportsmanship by Trudy angered Tracie. It gave her new inspiration. For Tracie, the next five slices were easier than the first. She would do everything in her power to win.

"Slice seventy-one is the breaking point," the

Porcine	(**pawr**-sahyn) – ADJ – pig-like; hoggish	
Cupidity	(kyoo-**pid**-i-tee) – N – strong desire	
Burgeoning	(**bur**-juhn-ing) – ADJ – growing and rapidly expanding	
Egregious	(i-**gree**-juhs) – ADJ – conspicuously bad	

announcer stated. "The last four watermelon eating competitions were decided on slice seventy-one."

The servers brought out extra large slices of watermelon and placed them before the two women. By merely looking at the giant watermelon slice, Tracie's remaining appetite began to *wane*. She hated the thought of losing, but she was unsure of her ability to finish it. Just the idea of giving victory to Trudy Jones motivated her. She knew that she could eat at least half of it. Tracie broke her slice in half. She started eating slowly, bite by bite. Through sheer determination, she finished the half. Tracie could feel watermelon overflowing her stomach all the way up her esophagus. She was done.

Trudy Jones, on the other hand, was still struggling to finish half. She put her slice down on her plate and quit. "It appears folks, that we have a tie because neither woman finished their slice! But that's not how we roll in Clarksville. Watermelon competition rules state that in case of such an occurrence, we will weigh the contestants' slices. The one with the lighter remaining portion wins!"

The servers brought out a scale. They placed Trudy's slice on the scale, removed it, wiped it off, then placed Tracie's slice. The servers whispered to the announcer. The crowd waited in anticipation for the results.

"The winner of this year's golden watermelon competition, by 2.5 grams, is Ms. Trudy Jones!"

"I win! I win!" she *vaunted* with pride. She walked up to the announcer, who handed her the golden watermelon statuette, and she posed for a picture.

Tracie stumbled over to her friends, nauseated. "I

Wane　　　　(weyn) – V – to decrease in size, extent, or degree
Vaunt　　　　(**vawn**-t) – V – to praise or boast about

never want to see a watermelon again. I feel so sick." she said. Sandra and Celeste got on both sides of her shoulders and carried her away from the pavilion. "Girls, will you please leave me here," Tracie requested. "I need to get some watermelon out of my system."

Tracie bent over and began to vomit. Sandra and Celeste left her in peace.

On the other side of the room, Trudy Jones hobbled to edge of the pavilion, slow but happy leaving her trophy on the stage. From a distance, the announcer called out to her, "Ms. Jones! You forgot the Golden Watermelon!"

"Keep it," she scoffed. "I've got plenty of statues. I don't want that cheap thing."

"But, Ms. Jones, you earned it."

Begrudgingly, Trudy returned to the stage and picked up her award.

"I won," she responded. "That's all that matters."

Seeing a small trash bin away from the stage, Trudy carelessly tossed the trophy inside as walked away from the competition.

WORD REVIEW

Antedate	Elusive	Purvey
Augur	Emaciation	Quizzically
Boons	Empower	Singular
Burgeoning	Glibly	Tepid
Charily	Herald	Vagary
Conversant	Incongruous	Vaunt
Cupidity	Jostle	Vie
Desist	Nostrum	Wane
Dichotomy	Perquisites	Yen
Diffidence	Porcine	
Egregious	Promulgate	

12

The large group around the pavilion attracted the attention of Nick Franklin, who had just arrived at the park. In the middle of the crowd stood Mrs. Trudy Jones, waving her hands in the air and bragging to her friends.

Suddenly, the air surrounding him became *vitiated* by disgusting cigarette smoke. Nick turned to see Ryan, with Misty at his side, lighting up with a book of Flamingo Casino matches. Ryan took a few puffs. The smoke continued to *waft* in Nick's direction. Recognizing his peers, Nick decided to make conversation.

"Hey, guys! What's going on?" Nick asked.

"Misty, do you hear something?" Ryan refused to *deign* low enough to respond to Nick.

"Stop that!" Misty said as she slapped him on the back of the head. She looked at Nick. "It's the watermelon-eating contest. Tracie just lost. She lasted seventy slices. She really wanted that trophy."

"Wow, that's amazing. Poor Tracie, though. Well, I guess I'll be going," said Nick awkwardly.

"Yeah, maybe you should," Ryan responded, and

Vitiate	(**vish**-ee-eyt) – V – to debase or lower in moral or aesthetic status
Waft	(waft) – V – to move or go lightly on
Deign	(deyn) – V – to condescend in order to give or offer something

again received another slap.

Nick wandered off into the park, alone with his thoughts. At one point, he had wanted to fit in with the cool kids. He'd wanted to be popular. Not anymore. His countless experiences with Ryan and other bullies *extirpated* any longing he had ever had to get along with them. He didn't *want* to be Ryan's friend, even if he could. Nick had been saving the rest of his money for the beginning of the school year, hoping that by buying nice things he could somehow jostle his way into the higher social circle. Now, he didn't want to impress them by any forms of inveiglement. He could not care less.

Tomorrow, Nick was going to get some money from Mr. Bering and start spending on what made him happy. Forget new clothes and cool accessories! He wanted to buy furniture for his house. No more saving to make a bang at the first day of school. He was going to forget the people who brought him down once and for all.

As he walked through the celebration, Nick was suddenly hit in the face with a plastic bag. He took in several gasping breaths, and removed the litter from his face as quickly as possible. A little embarrassed, he quickly surveyed the scene to make sure nobody had noticed, and as usual, nobody paid any attention to him. Disheartened, he took the trash to a waste bin beside the pavilion. Inside, he found the Golden Watermelon trophy. With a smile, he picked it up and put it in his backpack. *Maybe he could help somebody else have a better Fourth of July?*

When it came about time for the Joe Harrington concert, Nick headed for the stage. Fortunately for him, Mr. Bering had offered him a seat at the front. He was

---

Extirpate   (**ek**-ster-peyt) – V – to destroy completely

guaranteed a good spot because the Berings always had the front row. It felt good to have friends in high places. Nick also relished in the knowledge that someday he, too, would be a lawyer and receive the perks that Mr. Bering had.

He found the Berings on the first row, just as he had expected. Sandra and Celeste were sitting on the left, Mr. and Mrs. Bering on the right. There was a seat saved between them. Nick sat between Celeste and Mr. Bering. Some local alternative rock group was performing, but no one seemed interested in it.

"I'm glad you could make it," Mr. Bering said with a smile.

"I'm glad to be here," Nick replied.

"What's up, Nick?" asked Celeste.

"Nothing much," he responded, "just enjoying the summer."

"Good," she replied. "I'm glad to hear it." Celeste returned to her conversation with Sandra.

Nick tried to watch the rock group, but he quickly lost interest. He was just starting to get bored when the mayor came onstage to announce the main act. Mayor Hill walked to the microphone with spring in his step, excited to have his town's ceremony go off so well. The audience was huge, and he was aware that most were possible voters who would recognize the tremendous job his office did in preparing this event. He carried in his hand a plaque with a key on it.

"Thank you one and all for coming to our Fourth of July extravaganza!" he shouted. "Are y'all proud to be Americans?"

The crowd roared back in response.

"Now before I take the liberty to introduce our headliner tonight, I would like to take some time to talk about one of my dearest and closest friends. It's somebody that you all know, but don't realize it—somebody who has an *impeccable* spirit of gift-giving. This man has spent the entire summer searching people who need blessings. Bicycles, cars, new books for our library—no one has been more generous to our town."

Nick began getting nervous. *Had Mr. Bering told the mayor his identity?* He began to sweat. He looked over at Mr. Bering, who winked at him. The wink was very *equivocal*, and it confused Nick even more.

"By his personal request to me," Mayor Hill continued. "I have promised to keep him anonymous, so from now on I will refer to him as the Summer Santa. I find it very humble for him not to want to be recognized for these acts of generosity. However, not intending to *lionize* him, I would like to present to him this key, engraved with the name of the Summer Santa. This key represents the great service and commitment he has given to our community. I'll hang it in City Hall to encourage others to commit to similar good works and charity. Now, I want y'all to give a round of applause to this gentleman because he's here in our midst." The audience cheered. "With that said, let's get this show started! I now present to you Joe Harrington!"

The sound of a band began to play, and the lead singer jumped onto the stage. The crowd screamed with excitement.

The mayor's speech sent two heads spinning in thought. Nick appreciated the mayor's kindness. He

Impeccable	(im-**pek**-uh-buhl) – ADJ – free from fault or blame; perfect
Equivocal	(i-**kwiv**-uh-kuhl) – ADJ – of uncertain nature or classification
Lionize	(**lahy**-uh-nahyz) – V – to treat as an object of great interest or importance

thought about the *moniker*, Summer Santa. He kind of liked it. He was glad that his gift-giving spree could end in such a grand fashion. Nick was satisfied.

Celeste also began to think. She knew that the mayor could not be responsible for the summer gifts; he would have taken credit for them himself if he were. She would have to start right back at the beginning and again investigate the actions of her father. She was sure that the Summer Santa was someone very close to him, someone she would normally overlook. Maybe the Summer Santa was one of his best friends. Celeste put her thoughts on hold when Joe Harrington began to sing his latest hit, "Don't Break my Heart with your High-heeled Shoe." She got up and screamed in jubilation.

Harrington's performance was flawless. He ended his set with "Help Somebody Down," a *poignant* song about a grandmother who spent her life serving others. Celeste sat down in her chair next to Nick.

"You know, it's really cool what that Santa guy did for our town," she said. "I've wanted to figure out who he is for quite some time just for personal reasons, but now I think I want to meet him if for no other reason than to thank him for what he's done. I bet he's a really nice guy."

"You never know; you may already be friends with him," Nick replied.

"No way. None of my friends are *that* nice! But I think I could be his friend."

The song ended then and Harrington began to sing "God Bless America." As he sung the high notes in

---

Moniker   (**mon**-i-ker) – N – nickname
Poignant   (**poin**-yuhnt) – ADJ – apt; touching

the climax of the song, a *cascade* of fireworks flashed in the sky. The whole experience was so moving that Nick's eyes began to water. He was so overwhelmed by his blessings. He knew that because he was blessed, he needed to bless others. Nick quickly wiped his eyes and hoped nobody had noticed.

Cascade   (kas-**keyd**) – N – something falling or rushing forth in quantity

WORD REVIEW

Cascade   Impeccable   Vitiate
Deign   Lionize   Waft
Equivocal   Moniker
Extirpate   Poignant

13

Nick walked through his penthouse, pad and paper in hand. He had several items on his agenda today. The first was to make an itemized list of repairs and supplies needed to make his house safe, comfortable, and livable. Then he had to decide on furnishings.

In each room, Nick took his sketchpad and drew a picture of what it would look like completely finished. These pictures would help him decide what he needed to buy. He didn't want to have any *extraneous* costs, so he planned very carefully.

For the house's actual structure, he would get a new roof and electricity run to it. For furnishings, he'd get a big couch and television in the game room. In the kitchen he would put a little table and some chairs. The library would be filled with bookshelves and books, and maybe also a desk and recliner. After all it was *imperative* that his favorite room be the most comfortable. The bedroom, of course, would need a bedroom set.

Nick decided to start spending secretly on his house first because he didn't want his mother to notice his

Extraneous	(ik-**strey**-nee-uhs) – ADJ – not essential or vital
Imperative	(im-**per**-uh-tiv) – ADJ – necessary; not to be avoided or evaded

aberrant expenditures until after all the money was gone. His Ferrari was obviously going to have to be the very last thing he bought.

Mr. Bering had given him all his money, except the money for his new car. Nick grabbed his backpack and his drawing to go shopping.

His first stop was the hardware store, which also doubled as the office of Handy Dan's Repair Services. Dan Farmer was probably the nicest, most skilled home repairman in Clarksville County. Nick knew that he could easily hire Dan to do the little repairs his home needed.

It was early in the day, so there were no other customers to distract Dan from being attentive to Nick. "Hey, Mr. Farmer," Nick said, "do you have some time available to do some repair work on my property outside of town?"

"Well let me see here," Dan said as he pulled out his work schedule. "I'll be free this weekend when Lily comes to take care of things here in the store. What type of service do you need?"

"The house needs an electric hookup and some outlets. It could also use a new roof."

"Well, I'll be happy to do the work. It will definitely take more than a day though."

"That's perfect. Can I pay you now?"

"Nobody ever does," he responded. "But I'm not going to stop you!"

Nick smiled and rifled through his backpack to grab his wad of cash. He counted out a down payment. "If you need any more," he added, "you know where to find me."

Aberrant	(uh-**ber**-uhnt) – ADJ – deviating from the usual or natural type

Nick walked out of the store, leaving behind a puzzled Mr. Farmer. He wondered where a kid Nick's age would get so much money. He was amused by this somewhat *droll* situation. Most kids Nick's age would be saving for a video game system or some other toy. Nick wanted home repairs. It was a very *precocious* decision for the mature young man. Mr. Farmer chuckled at the thought.

Close to the hardware shop was the furniture store, Nick's next stop. A big red sign on the front said, "Outrageous Summer Sale!" As he walked through the automatic glass doors, the cool breeze and faint odor of potpourri *evoked* in him a feeling of relaxation. The two salespeople approached him.

"Hello!" said Sally, "I'm Sally and this is Truman, and we're here to help you fulfill all your furnishing needs."

"What can we help you find today?" added Truman.

"Well, we're furnishing our house, and my mom is working today, so I'm here to pick out some stuff," Nick said, shading the truth.

"In that case, let's get started," said Truman with big eyes full of excitement. He and Sally walked Nick over to the living room section.

"Here are our sofas and recliners," Sally said. "Each has a unique exquisite fabric. Some are made of pure leather."

Nick ran his hand along one of them; it felt like heaven. He began testing each one, sitting in the recliners and lying down on the couches. He considered his options for a while until finally picking a black leather sofa for his

---

Droll	(drohl) – ADJ – having a humorous, whimsical, or odd quality
Precocious	(pri-**koh**-shuhs) – ADJ – exceptionally advanced in development
Evoke	(i-**vohk**) – V – to call forth or up

game room. He also bought a brown leather recliner for his study.

The group moved to the kitchen area, where Nick picked out a four-seat dinette set perfect for small get-togethers. Nick was thrilled with his decisions so far.

The *ambience* of the bedroom section was palace-like. Royal beds with curtains and ruffles and bedspreads made of silk and other luxurious fabrics were dispersed about the room. Nick felt regal simply being there. He picked out a bedroom set made of cherry wood and a mattress with a topper made of goose feathers. He loved it.

Sally and Truman then took him to the office section to find bookshelves for his library. Large wooden desks with professional chairs to accompany them made it the *apotheosis* of how a study room should appear. Nick wanted his study to be exactly like this section of the furniture store. He ordered everything, only on a smaller scale to fit the inside of his penthouse.

Nick wandered around the store some more and picked up odds and ends—lamps, rugs, and a few decorative pieces—and then headed to pay. Sally was shocked when he handed her a stack of bills at the cash register. "Your mother sure knows how to send you shopping," she said.

"Do y'all deliver?" Nick asked. Sally and Truman both giggled *inanely* at the question.

"Were you planning on carrying this stuff home?" Truman responded. They both began to giggle again. Nick

Ambience	(**am**-bee-uhns) – N – a feeling or mood associated with a particular place, person, or thing (Note: also ambiance)
Apotheosis	(uh-poth-ee-**oh**-sis) – N – the perfect example
Inanely	(i-**neyn**-lee) – ADV – lacking significance, meaning, or point

returned their laughs with a polite smile. He gave them the address to his penthouse and left the store.

All this shopping had made Nick extremely tired, but he couldn't give up yet. He still had more to do. The mall was his next stop, and if he found everything, hopefully it would be his last. It was time to buy personal items. First, he went to Gringo Brothers to buy some clothes that were "el frio" (aka cool) as the store clerks said. Gringo Brothers specialized in customer service, so immediately upon entering, Nick was met by Amy, his new personal shopping assistant.

"Casual, formal, beach—where do you need clothes for?" she asked.

"Everywhere," he responded.

"Oh, well then we'd better get started right away!"

They headed for the casual section first. Amy started grabbing clothes off the shelves and piling them in his hands. "You're going to need a pair of nice jeans for parties, holey jeans for school, dark jeans for when you wear a light shirt, light jeans for when you wear a dark shirt, and a pair of versatile jeans for when all the others are dirty. Then you need some designer T-shirts in every color, especially pink—it's back in style." Amy continued to give suggestions and hand a helpless Nick more clothes.

"OK," she replied. "You're going to need a few pairs of dress pants—khaki, black, and gray—several button downs, and an assortment of ties." By the time Amy had piled all these items in Nick's overloaded hands, his face was hidden behind the *apex* of the pile. "Can I try these on?" his muffled voice sounded from behind the clothes.

"Of course! Right this way." Amy led him to the dressing rooms. Nick closed the door. The jeans he had been

---

Apex   (**ey**-peks) – N – the highest point

given were much tighter than the ones he was used to wearing. He loved the T-shirt, though. It made him look buff and cool all at the same time. He opened the door to show Amy.

Wow, you look good!" she said. "You should definitely keep both of those." She handed Nick another set of clothes, and he gave her the clothes that he had been wearing when he walked into the store. She smiled at his fresh appearance and then looked at his well-worn, old clothes with ***antipathy***. "You may have worn these in here, but you're definitely not wearing them out." She held them far away from her nose as if some sort of ***malodor*** was originating from them. "I'll go put these in a bag," she said with a look of disgust.

Nick continued trying on clothes. He was surprised at how much his appearance changed by simply altering the style of his clothes. Of course Amy liked everything that he tried on, but Nick was only sold on a few of the items that were selected. In the end, he kept the basics: a few T-shirts, two pairs of jeans, a pair of khaki pants, and a dress shirt and tie. He paid for these purchases, and then moved on to search for sunglasses. To be truthful, Nick didn't have the slightest clue what styles of sunglasses were cool. He only knew that he needed a pair to complement his car.

When he arrived at the Sunglass Emporium, the sales clerk could tell by the expression on his face that he was desperately in need of help.

"Looking for some shades?" the clerk asked.

"Yeah," Nick told him, "but I don't know where to start."

"First, do you have a price range?"

"Well, whatever it costs to get a pair to match a Ferrari."

"That answers my question," he said. "Let's look at

Antipathy   (an-**tip**-uh-thee) – N – settled aversion or dislike
Malodor   (mal-**oh**-der) – N – an offensive odor

these." The clerk took Nick over to the section of ultra-trendy sunglasses, and then selected a few pairs for Nick's consideration. Nick began to try them on. The first had circular lenses and the straps hooked to his forehead instead of his ears. They made him look like a bug. The second pair was one solid rectangular lens, and it reminded Nick of Star Trek. "Do you have any that are less... experimental?" Nick asked.

"Of course," the clerk responded. He took Nick to the classy section.

Nick put on several pairs, but none looked quite right. He looked through the sunglasses displays in search of something spectacular. Finally, he found a pair of Aviators. "I think I'll try these on," he said.

"Certainly," the clerk responded. Nick placed them on his head. It was a perfect match.

"Those look good on you!" the clerk *adulated* him.

"I'll take them!" Nick said. He paid the salesclerk. Now he had only one thing left to do, and this was the best thing of all: shop for his mom. Sarah Franklin was the most hardworking, diligent woman that he knew. The idea of buying her presents made him happy. She was so *provident* with her money that she never lavished herself with nice gifts and things like that. She always bought her clothes at discount stores on sale. Well today, Nick was going to buy her all the things she wanted, but would never buy for herself.

He started at the shoe store. His mom walked around all day on her feet, so it was *requisite* that he buy her the most comfortable pair of shoes that existed. The

---

Adulate	(**aj**-uh-leyt) – V – to flatter; praise
Provident	(**prov**-i-duhnt) – ADJ – frugal
Requisite	(**rek**-wuh-zit) – N – essential; necessary

salesperson got him a pair of gelatin-soled tennis shoes, built for comfort. He knew this was the pair that his mom needed. Then Nick went searching for perfume. The lady at the in-store boutique allowed Nick to smell every scent available. The scents all began to blend and send Nick into a state of dizziness. The lady continued to spray perfume in his face until he finally selected the one that smelled the least like chemicals and boutiques. When he left there, he headed for the jewelry store. He picked out a nice set of gold pearl earrings he knew she would love. They were exactly her style—simple and elegant.

Nick was more than satisfied with the entire day of shopping. He had accomplished a lot. Finally, he had spent all his excess money. All he had left to do was buy his car and surprise his mom.

Nick dreamed about how he would spring the news. He knew that it had to be extremely elaborate, like maybe a great big birthday surprise for her. He would have to wait only until the end of July, and he had already kept the secret for so long, a few more weeks would be easy.

First, he would wrap the pair of shoes in a box and have them delivered to his mom by a coworker with a note that read, "Hi, Mom, these are for you. Expect more surprises when you get home." She would put them on and feel glorious as she walked all day. Her mind would be racing, wondering what other things could be waiting for her.

After work, she would find no one home. There would be only a note attached to another wrapped box containing the perfume. This note would say, "Come outside and wait for me." She'd stand in the doorway looking for him, and not even recognize him as he pulled up in front of the house in his hot new Ferrari. She would walk up to the car in shock. In her seat the box of pearl earrings would be waiting for her. At this point, she might even cry. Then she would stop and wonder where the money came from, and she might even get angry. He would then explain to her where he found it and what he'd been doing with it. The story would definitely test her *credulity* being so fantastic and unbelievable. She might cry some more after that.

They would drive to his penthouse, a place she had been many times before, but this time she would be totally surprised by its appearance. The new white paint *veneer* on the outer walls would captivate her. She would get out and see the freshly watered lawn, and be so proud of the care that her son had taken on his property.

When she opened the door, the sight of the brand new furniture would overwhelm her. She'd go into every room and be totally excited about the decorations and appearance, asking questions about the origins of the furniture and how he thought of such unique ideas. They would walk into the kitchen and on the table would be a big white birthday cake. She would again hug him and cry. Then they'd celebrate together by eating cake and discussing how Nick was able to keep such a wonderful secret. If there was any money left over, he would give it to her as the rest of her present.

It would be the best birthday she'd ever had.

Credulity	(kruh -**dyoo**-li-tee) – N – readiness or willingness to believe especially on slight or uncertain evidence
Veneer	(vuh-**neer**) – N – a protective or ornamental facing

WORD REVIEW

Aberrant	Credulity	Malodor
Adulate	Droll	Precocious
Ambience	Evoke	Provident
Antipathy	Extraneous	Requisite
Apex	Imperative	Veneer
Apotheosis	Inanely	

14

Ryan awoke on the couch in the living room of his dad's apartment.

"This is *libel!*" he heard his dad shout on the phone. "I want a written apology in the next edition of the paper." The phone slammed on the receiver.

Ryan sat up, confused. Tom Finley walked over to his son and showed him the latest edition of the newspaper. There was a full-page advertisement on the second page for Pete's Plumbing. "Pete's Plumbing," it read. "Better than the local guy."

"That local guy is me!" he shouted. "This is an *affront* to my business, as if it weren't slow enough already."

"Dad, I'm sure it's just a saying. I don't think they're trying to single you out."

"Nonetheless, *I* am the person this is talking about."

"Well, what do you want them to do about it?"

His dad paused in thought. "I want Pete's Plumbing to write an apology and *gainsay* the whole thing in the next advertisement!"

"They probably will," Ryan concluded. "They probably didn't even know who they were offending."

Libel	(**lahy**-buhl) – ADJ – defamation of a person by written or representational means
Affront	(uh-**fruhnt**) – N – a deliberate offense
Gainsay	(**geyn**-sey) – V – to declare to be untrue or invalid

Ryan got off the couch and went into the kitchen. He grabbed a bowl and box of cereal. "You eaten breakfast yet?" he asked his dad.

"Yeah, I got a sausage biscuit earlier."

Ryan nodded his head and poured himself a bowl. He ate Frosted Crisps for breakfast every day. He liked that the taste stayed the same—it was the one thing in his life that never changed.

"Well, I'm going to go to the office and wait for a job. Maybe today I'll have some work."

"Hey, Dad," Ryan said, "I'm going to look for a job again today. Then I can pitch in with the bills a little."

"Son, you know I would never make you do that."

"I know, but I want to," Ryan replied.

Tom Finley grabbed his lunchbox and headed out the door. Ryan watched him leave. He hated seeing his dad like this. His business was failing, and so he got irritated about everything. Ryan knew the Pete's Plumbing people didn't mean any harm in their advertisement. They were just trying to make a sale. He just wished that a main water line would break under the City Courthouse so his father could have something to do.

For several weeks Ryan had been looking for a job so he could help his dad out. He figured there must have been some sort of *collusion* between the fast food companies in town, because none of them wanted to hire him. At first, he thought that working in a job as low as fast food would be some sort of *ignominy*, but

---

Collusion   (kuh-**loo**-zhuhn) – N – secret agreement or cooperation especially for an illegal or deceitful purpose

Ignominy   (ig-**nom**-uh-nee) – N – deep personal humiliation and disgrace

because his search had proved fruitless, Ryan lowered his standards even further. He was going to try to help his dad in any way he could. Getting a degrading job was not that big of a sacrifice to make.

He just had to find one.

Ryan started up his black Corvette. Its engine began to purr. He loved that car. Driving it around town was his greatest joy and pleasure. It made him feel alive, like the king of the world. He could *slough* all his problems away and throw them out the window. Nobody could hurt him. His car was his world.

Ryan drove to the grocery store, hoping they were in need of a checker or a bagger or a stocker—anything. He parked and went inside. The place was like a ghost town. No checkers. No one in the aisles. It was completely empty. It was a confusing scene. Never before had he seen the place so dead.

As he walked through the store, Ryan called out, "Hello? Is anyone here?"

A noise came from the room upstairs. Ryan heard footsteps. Moments later, Saul Giovanni, the store's owner, met him on the floor.

"I'm sorry, sir. Italy is playing right now. I've been a bit distracted all day," he told Ryan.

"Oh, no problem at all. I'm Ryan Finley, and I came to apply for a job. Do you have any openings?"

"Listen, son," Giovanni said. "Business is slow right now. That's why I can spend the day watching television and not down here. We're already overstaffed." He sighed. "I'm sorry, but I just can't help you." Giovanni gave him a pat on the back.

Slough   (sluhf) – V – to cast off

Ryan tried not to look disappointed, but he was overcome. He walked out of the store in a state of utter sadness.

There was only one place left, and it was the most humiliating place of all: the mall. Everyone at his school went to the mall. Everyone would see him there. It was the *vogue* for kids at his high school to go to the mall and poke fun at everyone who worked there, especially people who went to the high school. Nothing would *sully* his reputation more than a lowly mall job.

But there was no way to avoid it; it was his ineluctable destiny.

Ryan developed a plan. He would walk around the entire mall, from one side to the other, filling out applications everywhere he went.

As he went through the mall doors, he was met by Nick, who was loaded down by shopping bags.

"Hey, Ryan," Nick ventured hesitantly.

"Doing some shopping, Nicholas?"

"Yeah, just buying some clothes and some gifts. Nothing much."

"Well aren't *you* cool," Ryan responded sarcastically.

"Uhh, well, I'm going to head out. I'll see ya."

Nick walked away. Ryan watched as he struggled to open the doors with his full hands. It angered him to see Nick. It wasn't fair that he would have enough money to buy so much stuff. He hated the fact that he had to get a demeaning job. *Life was so unfair.* This attitude ruined his first interview.

Vogue	(vohg) – N – popular currency, acceptance, or favor; popularity
Sully	(**suhl**-ee) – V – to make soiled or tarnished

"Why do you want to work at Clothing Factory?" the interviewer asked.

"I don't really want to work at Clothing Factory. I just need some money."

Ryan was dismissed, and he left the store angry at himself for messing it up. He moved from store to store, turning in applications right and left. His attitude improved, but he was still unable to get anything.

Eventually he came to the very last shop in the entire mall, Surf World. He was interviewed by the junior manager, Valerie.

"Have you applied at anywhere else in the mall?"

"Everywhere else, except the girly stores. I can only stoop so low."

"What can you bring to the Surf World team that sets you apart from other applicants?"

"I think I bring a new perspective to the clothing world," Ryan said. "I know a whole lot about people who don't keep up with the current trends. I know how they think, and I know how to sell to them."

After a few more questions, Valerie thanked him for his interview. "We will keep in touch," she said.

Ryan could tell he was being dismissed. He couldn't let that happen. "This interview is not over," Ryan said *intransigently*. "This store is my last hope of a job, and I have the *competence* needed to do everything that will be required of me here. Please, hire me," he begged.

Intransigently	(in-**tran**-si-juhnt-lee) – ADV – characterized by refusal to compromise or to abandon an extreme position or attitude
Competence	(**kom**-pi-tuhns) – N – sufficiency of means for the necessities and conveniences of life; capability

"To be honest," Valerie responded. "You have no work experience and no references. You are a student, which means as soon as school starts, you'll quit. We just don't go about hiring people in your situation."

"Valerie," Ryan said. "I need this job. I will *not* quit when school starts, and do I really need work experience to sell clothing? I think I can handle it."

Valerie gave him a once-over and sighed. "Let me go talk to the senior supervisor." She excused herself and walked off in search of her coworker. In the distance, Ryan watched Valerie meet with a middle-aged man in a suit. They appeared to be discussing him very passionately. Ryan just had to wait. He was sitting in the middle of the store. He watched the customers browse through the merchandise hanging up and on shelves. He was watching the people walk outside the store when he recognized Sandra and Tracie. Sandra noticed him too.

"Tracie!" said Sandra. "I think that's Ryan inside Surf World."

They both stopped in their tracks.

"I wonder what he's doing here," Tracie added.

"Surely, he's not applying for a job. He said he would never '*degrade*' himself enough to work in a mall."

"Let's go check it out."

Tracie and Sandra walked to the entrance of the store and waved at Ryan, who smiled, red-faced. The girls came closer, but stopped when they saw the two managers approaching him.

"Ryan," said the senior manager, Troy Carey. "I would like to have a word with you."

Ryan stood up from his spot and said, "Yes sir."

Degrade　　(di-**greyd**) – V – to lower in grade, rank, or status

"It appears as though you'd like a job here at Surf World. Is that correct?"

"Yes sir," he responded. "Very much so."

"Well Valerie and I are in a very different state of opinion on this," he said. "I think we should dismiss you, like we do with all the other candidates of your quality. Valerie seems to have a *heterodox* belief in you, while I, of course, cling to more traditional standards. She is willing to put you on here full-time. Well, because I don't want to hire you at all, we've come to a compromise, a *dialectical* decision. I've combined her full-time with my no time, which basically means a part-time job for you. Will you accept it?"

"Of course," Ryan replied and shook Mr. Casey's hand excitedly.

"Good, you start tomorrow. Go with Valerie to the back and she'll get you all the paperwork."

"Thank you so much, Mr. Casey."

Valerie and Ryan went to the back room. Sandra and Tracie looked at one another, overcome with mirth. They started to giggle.

"Can you imagine macho Ryan working here?" Tracie asked.

"I know! He's the one who always makes fun of mall employees."

They continued to chat until Ryan returned to the front of the store. He said good-bye to his new coworkers and walked over to the girls with a handful of documents.

Heterodox	(**het**-er-uh-doks) – ADJ – contrary to an acknowledged standard, a traditional form, or an established religion
Dialectical	(dahy-uh-**lek**-ti-kuhl) – ADJ – coming to a conclusion by merging two opposing views

"What are you girls doing here?" he asked.

"The better question," said Tracie, "is what are *you* doing here?"

"I just got a job," he replied.

"Aren't you the one who said, 'I would never work at the mall, even if my life depended on it.'?" Sandra asked.

"Why would I say that?" Ryan replied, pretending to forget his *erstwhile* statement. "That's a very ignorant thing to say."

"Whatever, big shot," Tracie said. "You can't fool us. But this will be good for you. You need to learn the good old-fashioned values of work."

"We're going to Frosty Crème," Sandra said. "Do you want to come?"

"Sure," he responded.

The threesome walked out of the mall together. Ryan was relieved. He had finally found a way to help his dad with the bills. Maybe it was a little degrading, but it didn't matter. Ryan was excited to be able to do something good for somebody other than himself for once. It seemed very uncharacteristic and foreign, but he was actually enjoying it. Who knew that doing nice things would make him feel so good?

The next day, Ryan realized why he had said such terrible things about mall jobs. Surf World was a horrible place to work. There was no way he could have *fathomed* just how bad this place was before actually experiencing it. Both his managers, Troy and Valerie, were absolutely insane.

His first assignment, two hours before the store

Erstwhile	(**urst**-wahyl) – ADJ – former; previous
Fathom	(**fath**-uhm) – V – to penetrate and come to understand

opened, was to replace all the fitting room clothes back on the racks. It seemed simple enough—until he saw the four barrels of unfolded clothes waiting for him. Ryan quickly began to run around the store searching for the location of the items in his first barrel. When he found one, he would carefully fold the item and **nest** it among similar ones. It took him an hour just to finish one barrel. He hadn't even finished the second one when the store opened and customers began to flood in.

Immediately Troy shouted at him, "Quit putting clothes back and start helping customers!"

Ryan replaced the barrel in the back and began greeting customers. "Welcome to Surf World, do you need any help?" he asked, over and over. He sounded like a mimicking parrot. The first person to actually want help, or at least someone to yell at, was an *irascible* middle-aged woman.

"How may I be of service?" he asked.

"It's about time someone stopped to help me! I have been waiting here looking stupid for over five minutes."

"I'm sorry ma'am. What can I do for you?"

"Is it true that your ultra-stretch jeans contain nylon in their fabric? Because I'm allergic to nylon, and I don't want to be itching when I wear them."

"Well, ma'am, I'm not sure. I'm sorry."

"Just my luck," she interrupted him. "Out of all the store employees, I get the idiot."

"I'm sorry, ma'am. I'm new here. But I'll go get my supervisor to help you."

Ryan canvassed the store for someone to help him.

Nest	(nest) – V – to pack compactly together
Irascible	(i-**ras**-uh-buhl) – ADJ – marked by hot temper and easily provoked anger

He spotted Valerie at the front. "Valerie, the woman over there needs help with fabric information." Ryan pointed to the irritated lady.

"What are you doing helping customers? There are barrels of clothes in the back that need to be replaced. I don't want to see you doing anything but replacing those clothes! Get to it!"

Ryan returned to the barrel he was working on and went back out to the front of the store. He hustled to put the clothes away as quickly as he could. Troy spotted him and walked to his barrel. He grabbed it and dumped it on the floor.

"Do you realize how unprofessional it looks when you replace clothes during store hours?" he said. "These barrels look ridiculous. I want you to take all these clothes back to the back and fold them. Come out with only several items at a time and continue this process until you're finished." He scowled. "If you wouldn't have been so *lackadaisical* this morning, you would already be done."

Ryan returned to the back with the big pile of clothes in his hands. He walked past the dressing room and saw a whole new barrel of clothes waiting for him. His mind-numbing job seemed *interminable*. He started folding. Eventually, he got into a rhythm and started moving really fast. His work was interrupted by Valerie's presence.

"What are you doing back here?" she *harried* him. "Putting up clothes is all well and good, but not when we need you in the front. We're short on salespeople because you are back here goofing off. Get out there and start selling!"

Lackadaisical	(lak-uh-**dey**-zi-kuhl) – ADJ – lacking life, spirit, or zest
Interminable	(in-**tur**-muh-nuh-buhl) – ADJ – having or seeming to have no end
Harry	(**har**-ee) – V – to harass; to worry or annoy

He quickly found a customer who needed help. Fortunately, this one was a friendly girl his age.

"I'm just looking for an outfit for this weekend, and I need some advice."

Ryan was glad to have found a problem that he could solve. The girl showed him two outfits. One was a bright green halter-top coupled with a pair of jeans. The other was a black skirt paired with a designer T-shirt.

"Honestly," Ryan said. "I would go with the jeans and halter. It's nice, but casual enough that you could wear the outfit anywhere."

"That's what I was thinking," the girl said. "I just needed a second opinion. Thanks!"

Ryan roamed around the store looking for people who needed help making decisions. When he found them, he took pride in being able to give them some advice. When he found customers with other more difficult questions, he sent them to his supervisors. Ryan soon became comfortable with his job. He could *definitely* handle picking out clothes for customers.

By the time Ryan's shift was over, he was exhausted, but satisfied in having done a full day's work. He had accomplished a feat that not many of his high school friends would do. Working was not as bad as people cracked it up to be.

Ryan was folding clothes in the front when he was called to the back by Troy. "Ryan, could you come here please?" The sound of his voice *presaged* a bad encounter. As Ryan arrived at his location, Troy began his speech.

Presage   (**pres**-ij) – V – to give an omen or warning of

"Ryan, you're a really nice kid," he said **condescendingly**. "You have a good attitude, but I am wondering if you did any real work today. I'm standing here, looking at this big pile of clothes, and I'm asking myself, 'What happened to my new employee who was supposed to take care of this?' All day customers kept coming to me and asking me questions that they had already asked you. It was ridiculous! I don't know if you have what it takes to work at Surf World. I know you tried really hard today, but it just didn't cut it."

Ryan was blown away. He thought that he had done a good job, and he knew that he had worked extremely hard, even if Troy didn't see it. He left the store **discomfited** by the entire embarrassing experience. All he wanted to do was help his dad, and he couldn't even do that right. Ryan looked for a pay phone. He called Misty.

"Honey, what are you doing?"

"Oh, hey, Ryan. I'm just chilling at my house."

"Do you want to go out tonight?"

"Go out where?"

"I don't know. I just want to see you."

"Sure, I'll be waiting for you," she said.

"I'm on my way."

Ryan hung up the phone. Misty was the best girlfriend he had ever had. She was gorgeous and smart— everything a girlfriend was supposed to be. Right now, though, all he needed was a friend. He wanted someone to talk about his day. He couldn't tell his dad. It would make him even more depressed.

Ryan's black Corvette pulled up in front of Misty's

Condescendingly	(kon-duh-**sen**-ding-lee) – ADV – patronizingly; degradingly
Discomfit	(dis-**kuhm**-fit) – V – to put into a state of perplexity and embarrassment

house. He honked its horn and she came out the front door.

"I'll be back before midnight," she said, waving to her parents. She walked over to the car and opened the passenger door, giving Ryan a peck as she sat down. Her long brown hair was curled and she wore a cute black dress. Ryan stared at her, entranced by her beauty.

"If you stare too hard, your eyes will pop out," she said to him, smiling.

He put the car in gear and began to drive. Ryan looked forward, unable to say anything. He was thinking too much.

"You sounded upset on the phone," she said.

"I got laid off today," he used this ***euphemism*** to make getting fired sound less terrible.

"You had a job?" she asked. "Since when?"

"Today, and only today…I was just trying to help my dad out with some bills. Some good I am."

"I'm sure he would appreciate the gesture, Ryan," Misty responded.

"Do you think I can tell him that I got fired? It would make him feel bad for me, and then he'd be even more depressed."

Misty thought for a minute. "Maybe you should surprise him with your paycheck. Then he'll be so happy about getting the money, he'll forget about your getting fired."

"I don't know how happy he'll be with fifty bucks, but I'm sure it will help ***allay*** his disappointment."

A smile came across Ryan's face. Misty was the only

Euphemism	(**yoo**-fuh-miz-uhm) – N – the substitution of an agreeable or inoffensive expression for one that may offend or suggest something unpleasant
Allay	(uh-**ley**) – V – subdue or reduce in intensity or severity

facet of his life that made any sense. He looked deep into her eyes, enamored by her presence.

"Why am I so lucky?" he said.

"I wouldn't call getting fired lucky," she responded.

"No, I mean about you."

"God must feel bad about all the other rotten things in your life. I mean really, really bad," she said jokingly.

"I guess you're right…You are my blessing."

Ryan drove the car downtown, frustrated at himself for taking Misty for granted so often. He didn't treat her even close to the way she deserved to be treated. Right then and there, he made a firm decision to be the kind of boyfriend she needed. He rolled down the windows and turned up his radio. The two began to cruise the square. On weekends, there would be many other cars doing the same thing, but there was no one else out that night. The streetlights turned green every time they drove through them. They began counting how many they could pass through without stopping for a red light.

It was amazing to just enjoy each other's company. The air felt cool as it flowed through the windows. The city looked so beautiful in the light of the moon. Ryan felt like he could conquer the world. He had everything he needed: a beautiful girl by his side and a car that made him proud. Ryan felt content and happy. Sure it had its rough spots, but in all, his life was pretty good.

By the twenty-seventh time they passed the streetlight, it turned red. Ryan looked to his girlfriend in the warm red glow. Overwhelmed with emotions, he turned her face toward him and searched the beautiful depths of her eyes.

"I love you," he whispered.

Facet   (**fas**-it) – N – any of the definable aspects that make up a subject or an object

WORD REVIEW

Affront	Euphemism	Irascible
Allay	Facet	Lackadaisical
Collusion	Fathom	Libel
Competence	Gainsay	Nest
Condescendingly	Harry	Presage
Degrade	Heterodox	Slough
Dialectical	Ignominy	Sully
Discomfit	Interminable	Vogue
Erstwhile	Intransigently	

15

Two weeks later, Ryan went back to Surf World to pick up his paycheck. He walked into the store and found Valerie folding clothes. "Excuse me," he said. "I came to pick up my paycheck."

She looked up at him, irritated, as if she was being importuned by him. Without saying a word she walked over to the cash register. She placed her key in the drawer, opened it, and grabbed an envelope with this name on it.

"Thank you," he told her.

She glared at him. "You know, I went out on a limb for you. And quitting after one day was no way to repay me."

Ryan, realizing immediately that Valerie wasn't aware of his having been fired, defended himself.

"I didn't quit," he said. "Troy fired me."

Valerie looked surprised, then her eyes narrowed in anger and she clenched her fists. "That idiot! You know, we had a bet to see whether or not you were going to last. He won only because he cheated. I am so much better than he is," she said *superciliously*. Valerie then paused to cool herself. She looked at Ryan much more politely, "I'm sorry that you had to deal with him, but there's nothing I can do about it now. We've already replaced you. If you want a

---

Superciliously   (soo-per-**sil**-ee-uhs-lee) – ADV – patronizingly haughty

job somewhere else, put my name down and I'll give you a good reference."

"Thanks, I appreciate it."

Valerie smiled at Ryan, and he walked out of the store. His self-confidence was somewhat restored. Maybe with a good reference, he could get another job. Things began to look up. Now, when he told his dad the story, he wouldn't have to say he was fired because of a poor work ethic. He could just simply tell him about the supervisor infighting, and how happy he was to be rid of the whole situation.

Ryan drove home, excited to give his dad the check and tell him the surprising news. When he arrived, however, his dad's car was gone. Ryan went into the house to grab a snack. He got out a jar of peanut butter and a banana, and then combined the two into one glorious sandwich. As he ate, he thought about how he was going to tell his father.

"Here's my first paycheck," he would say, and then his dad would look at him in surprise and shock.

"You got a job?" he would ask.

Then Ryan would say, "I had one, but I got fired after one day. It wasn't my fault though." Ryan would tell him the whole story about the day of work, then tell him that Valerie would give him a reference, so there was a good chance he could get another better job. His dad would thank him for the money, and then encourage him to keep up the good work. The conversation would be glorious, too, just like his sandwich.

Ryan stuffed the rest of his snack in his mouth and headed back out to his car. He couldn't wait for his dad to come home, so he decided to go to his office to meet him.

Ryan arrived at the headquarters of Bloomington Plumbing a little before five o'clock. In his excitement, he burst through the office doors. He found his dad sitting in his work chair, his face pale and wrinkled with *woe*. Ryan's eagerness died. He suddenly became frightened.

His dad looked at him. "The doctor called," he said. "I have cancer."

"*What?*" Ryan responded in shock. "That's impossible! Totally impossible."

"Well," his dad said, barely able to continue, "apparently there has been a tumor *encroaching* on my brain for some time."

Ryan couldn't accept this. "You're going to be OK, though, right? They can fix it."

His dad sighed. "There's a surgery, but I'd have to go all the way to Chicago to get it done. We can't afford it. I think it's too late; it may already be *irrevocable* anyway."

"No, Dad! We are *not* going to give up like this! I'm sure there's something we could do."

Ryan was stunned. His entire life was crashing down on him. His father was dying.

Everything seemed so meaningless. Money, friends, jobs—none of it mattered in the slightest. Forget paying bills! Forget everything. He was caught in a place where death stood juxtaposed to life. Eternity was a foot away from him. Nothing material meant anything.

"Son," his father ventured hesitantly, "I would never ask this of you unless it was absolutely necessary."

"What is it, Dad? I'll do anything."

"I'm going to need to sell your car."

Woe	(woh) – N – a condition of deep suffering from misfortune, affliction, or grief
Encroach	(en-**krohch**) – V – to advance beyond the usual or proper limits
Irrevocable	(i-**rev**-uh-kuh-buhl) – ADJ – not possible to revoke; unalterable

"Between your life and my car? I'd pick your life any day. You're having that surgery," Ryan said with finality.

"It's not for the surgery, Ryan," his dad said. "It's for my burial."

Ryan's eyes widened in absolute horror. His dad continued. "I thought I had a lot more time to save for that sort of thing, so I never did. I don't need a nice funeral, but even the cheapest casket is several thousand dollars. I can take the car down to Jerry's and get a good price on it."

Ryan kneeled in front of his dad and began to cry. "No! You're not going to die! I won't let you!" Tears poured down his face. His father embraced him as he began to weep.

"I'm sorry," he said. "I'm sorry that I have to leave you like this. It was never going to be my plan, of course. My business was going to pick up and I was going to send you to school. I'm…so sorry."

"Are you sure there's nothing we can do?"

"If we've caught the cancer in the *incipient* stage, then maybe there is a chance for survival with the surgery. No matter what, time will only *exacerbate* my worsening condition. There is no way we can find the money soon enough for it to even matter."

Ryan pulled away from his father, "You know what? This isn't fair. You are the most decent guy in this county. This should not happen to you."

"The Lord gives, and the Lord takes away," his father replied apathetically.

"Forget that!" Ryan responded defiantly.

Incipient	(in-**sip**-ee-uhnt) – ADJ – beginning to come into being or to become apparent
Exacerbate	(ig-**zas**-er-beyt) – V – to make more violent, bitter, or severe

He stormed out of the office, hopped into his car, and began to drive. His Corvette was the only thing that could possibly give him a hint of peace. A *myriad* of conflicting emotions filled his heart. His sadness had turned to anger—he was downright mad. He hated the stupid doctor for not discovering it sooner. He hated the dumb hospital because they charged too much money for life-saving surgeries. He hated God because it just simply was not fair. God was going to take away his father from him, simply out of spite.

Ryan lit up a cigarette to relieve the hatred and grief. How was he going to live without his father? What was he going to do? He already began to feel the emotional void opening in his soul. There would be a big, gaping hole forever inside him.

The only thing he could do was drive—drive until he felt better. He took the longest road he could find and just let himself go. His life was over.

The road turned to dirt, and Ryan drove off into the country. His emotions reawakened when he saw a familiar sight. In the distance was Nick's house. Ryan recognized it from the news blurb in the paper. It was a lot nicer now, with new paint and a new roof. He stopped his car in front of it.

Rage ignited in his soul. Thoughts about the injustice of the world filled him. There was very little difference between Ryan and Nick, but Nick didn't have a parent who was dying. He was living his life having a grand time, not having to worry about money or paying bills—or a dying father.

How could God allow the little snake to *expro-*

Myriad   (**mir**-ee-uhd) – N – a great number

priate some farmer's property for his own use? The farmer he stole from was probably a hard-working man, just like his dad.

Nick's actions were evil and *odious* to Ryan. He needed to teach Nick and God a lesson, one in fair play and justice.

Ryan put his Corvette in reverse and backed it up to the front of the house. He angrily got out of the car and slammed the door. Then he popped the trunk and rifled through its contents. He found an old water hose he had been meaning to take to the dump. Ryan cut off its metallic ends. He opened up the car's gas tank. He had just filled it up, and he didn't want Jerry at the car lot to get the use of his hard-earned gasoline, so he placed the hose in the tank. He sucked the other end until gas began to pour out.

He took pleasure in watering Nick's lawn with gasoline. When it sprayed on his new flowers, it made them wilt. It was fun to watch. Ryan began splashing all over the base of the house, then on the walls, then the windows, and finally the front door.

He could envision the whole structure in glorious flames. First the paint would peel off. Then the windows would turn black. The walls would have a light orange glow of smoke and *diaphanous* wisps of fire. Soon the roof would catch flame, and the sparks would crawl up to the apex of the house. He could see the shingles sag and eventually

---

Expropriate	(eks-**proh**-pree-eyt) – V – to deprive of possession or proprietary rights
Odious	(**oh**-dee-uhs) – ADJ – arousing or deserving hatred or repugnance
Diaphanous	(dahy-**af**-uh-nuhs) – ADJ – characterized by extreme delicacy of form; transparent

collapse into the rest of the structure.

Ryan pulled his hose out with enough gas left in his tank to get him home. He pulled his car far away from the building and left it idling. He walked back up to the house, which was now drenched in fuel. Lighting up another cigarette, he simply contemplated eternity. His life had become the closest to Hell that he could imagine. It was someone else's turn to feel the flames of injustice.

Ryan took his cigarette and threw it towards the house. A little fire started on the grass. It quickly spread. Soon it made contact with the building.

Ryan walked over to his car. He got in and took one last glance at his masterpiece of grief and pain. But his burning anger was merely fueled, not quenched. Ryan took his foot off the brake and drove away.

WORD REVIEW

Diaphanous
Encroach
Exacerbate
Expropriate

Incipient
Irrevocable
Myriad
Odious

Superciliously
Woe

16

The afternoon sun shone through the windows of Mr. Bering's office. As usual, his office was turned upside down, with papers and documents scattered everywhere. Nick sat in his usual chair, waiting for his final allotment of money.

"That's the last of it," Mr. Bering said. He handed Nick an eight-inch thick stack of bills equaling one hundred thousand dollars. Nick put the bundle in his backpack.

"Now when are you surprising your mother?" Bering questioned.

"Tomorrow afternoon," Nick replied.

"Well, if you want, I can drive you to Capital City tomorrow and help you pick out your Ferrari."

"I really would appreciate that. I don't know the first thing about buying a car."

"It's no problem," Bering said. "It's the least I can do to thank you for your *unsung* acts of anonymous kindness to our little town."

Nick shrugged. "All I did was share the gift that I was given."

"Well, you're the only teenager I know who would *abnegate* so much money to helping others rather than enriching your own life. And for that, I thank you." Mr.

Unsung	(uhn-**suhng**) – ADJ – not celebrated or praised
Abnegate	(**ab**-ni-geyt) – V – surrender; relinquish

Bering had the look of a proud parent, as if his son had just won the Little League championship or his daughter the regional science fair. He got up to shake Nick's hand, but was interrupted by the sound of fire engines roaring in the distance.

They both darted to the window. The noise had attracted a lot of attention downtown. The townspeople began to migrate toward the fire. Some ran outside of their shops, hopped in their cars, and followed the firefighters. A fire in Bloomington was a big deal, and everyone wanted to be on top of the news.

"I guess there's a fire," Bering said jokingly. "Do you want to go see it?" he asked Nick.

"Sure, let's go—I hope no one's hurt!"

Bering grabbed his suit jacket and walked out the door. Nick followed him downstairs to his car. They sped down Main Street.

Bering headed for the outskirts of town, but the road had already begun to fill up with cars. Soon, he had to stop completely. In the distance rose a visible cloud of thick black smoke.

"I wonder what type of fire it is," Nick queried.

"If we don't get through this *impasse*, we'll never find out," Bering replied. The car inched along the roadway. After a while, they noticed the road barricade. The car in front of them turned around and went back.

Bering pulled his car up to it. "Now it's time to use my super attorney powers," he said. Bering got out of the car and began talking to the police officer stationed at the roadblock. Nick watched as the cop nodded his head and

---

Impasse   (im-**pas**) – N – a predicament affording no obvious
escape

waved for Bering to pull through. He came back to the car, and the officer moved the barricade.

"What did you say to him?" asked Nick.

"If I told you, I would have to kill you," he responded.

As they continued on the road, they got closer and closer to the area where Nick's penthouse was located. He began to get nervous. He started to worry about his property, but denied the possibility to himself. His fear grew deeper, however, as they drove closer and closer to it.

When they passed Mrs. Ray's house and saw it unscathed by fire, Nick was relieved that she was safe, but he had a sinking feeling about his own land. When they saw his house in the distance, Nick was filled with horror.

It was engulfed by a cloud of smoke and flames.

The Clarksville County Volunteer Fire Department was standing near the building's exterior. They weren't spraying the house with water, just soaking the ground around it.

Nick jumped out of the car and ran toward his house. A firefighter caught him in the front yard. "I'm sorry, son. This situation is too **precarious** for you to get close to it and risk being hurt."

"But this is my house!" Nick screamed in desperation. "What happened to my house?!" He began to sob. "Why aren't you putting it out? *Why don't you try to put it out?*" Nick fell on the ground and wept. "*Why me?*" he screamed. "*Why me?!*"

This scene filled Mr. Bering with an overwhelming

Precarious   (pri-**kair**-ee-uhs) – ADJ – dependent on uncertain premises; dangerous sense of *pathos* for the disappointed young man. He approached the firefighter. "Why don't y'all put it out?" he asked him.

"Sir, it's the middle of the summer and we have a limited supply of water in this county. That house doesn't have a chance of surviving—we have to conserve the water we do have."

Nick knelt on the ground and watched his house burn. That was all he could do—watch it. His house would burn to the ground and nobody could stop it. Inside were his mom's gifts, his new clothes, all of his new furniture. All disappearing as quickly as it had come. For Nick, this disaster was *tantamount* to the end of the world.

"What caused the fire?" Bering asked the fireman.

"The *modus operandi* of the crime appears to be arson with gasoline as the fuel."

"What *dullard* would do such a stupid thing?" Bering asked in shock.

"There's no telling," the firefighter replied. "It could be random mischief. It could be a premeditated hate crime. There's really no way for us to know at this point. In the morning, Police Chief Briggs and the fire investigator are going to comb through the scene and search for evidence. They always come up with something."

Pathos	(**pey**-thos) – N – an emotion of sympathetic pity
Tantamount	(**tan**-tuh-mount) – ADJ – equivalent in value, significance, or effect
Modus Operandi	(**moh**-duhs op-uh-**ran**-dahy) – N – distinct pattern or method of operation that indicates or suggests the work of a single criminal in more than one crime
Dullard	(**duhl**-erd) – N – a stupid or unimaginative person

Mr. Bering was baffled. Who would do such a *wanton*, hateful act out of the blue? As town attorney, he had to worry about the culprits of this crime. It could be a message to the townspeople, some sort of symbol of things to come. He hoped he was wrong. He couldn't imagine the horrors of having a militant group in the city. Now he was scared. He went to his car and got out his phone. He called his wife.

"Honey, I'm outside of town with Nick. There's a big fire here, and the firefighters think it's arson. I want you to be on the lookout for any strange cars or people hanging around the house. If this thing happens again, I don't want it to be at our house...No there's nothing to get worried about. I just would rather be safe than sorry...Don't worry, just keep your eye out for suspicious behavior...I love you, too...OK 'bye."

Bering then called Mayor Hill. "Mr. Mayor," he said, "I just wanted to alert you of possible criminal activity. There's a fire outside town that the fire department has deemed arson. I just want you to be aware of the possible risks of future attacks...OK, I'll stop being paranoid. Thank you, Mr. Mayor. Good night."

The evening air became *turbid* with thick, black, swirling smoke. Nick sat in a stupor, watching the fire *depredate* his penthouse. In a few moments, the best thing about his childhood would be destroyed. All his sacred memories of freedom were being annihilated.

Wanton	(**won**-tn) – ADJ – having no just foundation or provocation
Turbid	(**tur**-bid) – ADJ – not clear or transparent because of stirred-up sediment or the like; clouded; opaque
Depredate	(**dep**-ri-deyt) – V – to plunder; ravage

Nick felt tired. The *ghastly* sight, smell, and sound of his house being consumed by flames overwhelmed his soul. He couldn't handle the feelings that were inside him. This house was his anchor. Without it, he could not survive. He was lost.

Nick rose from his position as the sun began to set. Mr. Bering put his hand upon Nick's shoulder and stood patiently behind him, which served to slightly *pacify* Nick's anguish. Nick appreciated Bering's faithfulness as a friend. He turned to him and said resolutely, "I'm ready to go."

"OK," Bering replied.

Nick felt strange. His face was damp with tears, and he had just lost the only thing that really belonged to him. But the strange thing was that he knew that somehow it would be OK. He would find a way to live through this loss. He was going to go home and start over again.

As he walked over to the car, he noticed something on the side of the road. Some neon-colored paper sat in the dirt.

"What's this?" he said as he reached down to pick up an empty Flamingo Casino matchbook.

"Did you find something?" Bering asked.

"No, just some trash," Nick responded as he placed it in his pocket. In a split second Nick's sorrow had transformed to anger.

He knew the culprit of this crime.

Ryan Finley—the only guy he knew who associated with the Flamingo Casino—was a dead man. Why he would do such a thing was a mystery to him, but he deserved death. For no reason, he had picked on Nick all

Ghastly	(**gast**-lee) – ADJ – terrifyingly horrible to the senses
Pacify	(**pas**-uh-fahy) – V – to quiet or calm; to bring to a state of peace

his life. Nick had sat back—even tried to be nice to him!—but this was the last straw.

It was time for payback.

Nick got into the car and Mr. Bering drove him to his house. When he walked into the house, his eyes were red and heavy, and his face was flush from crying. He had the scowl of a *rancor* that would last a lifetime. It looked like someone had hit him with a car, and then reversed to run him over again.

His mom was waiting for him. When she saw him, she ran over and gave him a huge hug. Nick thought that he was done crying, but as his mom held him, he started up again.

"It's not right," he whimpered.

"I know, honey," she responded.

"Why is the world so cruel?"

"I don't know. It's so sad, but there's nothing we can do about it; I've been in the *doldrums* all day."

"It's just so terrible."

"I know. Reverend Grey is having a midnight vigil in honor of Tom Finley, and I think we should go to it."

"Tom Finley?" Nick asked, surprised. "What's   he got to do with anything?"

"He has brain cancer," she responded, taken aback. "That's what you're upset about, right? They're having the prayer meeting tonight to raise money for his surgery."

"What?"

"There's some experimental surgery that could help, but there was no way he could afford it. It's like

---

Rancor	(**rang**-ker) – N – bitter deep-seated ill will
Doldrums	(**dohl**-druhmz) – N – a spell of listlessness or despondency

$100,000 or something unreal. If you didn't know, then why are you upset?"

"Mom! My penthouse burned down!"

She was stunned speechless for a full minute. "Honey," she said in shock as she reached over to embrace him again. "I had no idea! I'm *so* sorry!"

"It's OK," he responded. "I just need to go *lament* this loss in solitude." Nick walked over to his bedroom.

"I'll come and get you tonight when it's time for the vigil," his mom called after him.

Nick went into his room and shut his door. He lay down on his bed. So many thoughts roamed through his head, but he had no idea what to think. He knew Ryan Finley had set his house on fire; he knew that without a doubt. Nick's soul flamed with anger against him. He hated him. There was nothing good about him. If given the chance to kill him, he would take it. The guy had been nothing but a villain in Nick's life.

On the other hand, his dad was sick, and not only sick…he was dying. It wasn't his dad's fault that Ryan was mean. Nick knew Tom. He was a decent guy. He didn't deserve to die.

But Ryan did. If there was a surgery where you could transplant death from one person to another, Nick would definitely pay for it.

Nick groaned as he thought about the remainder of his money. What he had expected to be an exciting opportunity had become a *recondite* dilemma that simply made his life difficult. He knew that he was the only person

---

Lament   (luh-**ment**) – V – to express sorrow, mourning, or regret for often demonstratively

Recondite   (**rek**-uhn-dahyt) – ADJ – dealing with very profound, difficult, or abstruse subject matter

in town with the key to Tom Finley's survival. His Ferrari money could not go to a better use, but he hated the thought of helping Ryan. Allowing Ryan's dad to die would be the greatest form of revenge he could possibly inflict.

But it went against every *precept* of morality that Nick held true. Helping Ryan after such a terrible action seemed totally unfair. To be just, you cannot reward bad behavior, yet to be merciful, you cannot let another person suffer for the mistakes of others. It was right to be just and it was right to be merciful. He had come across a moral *paradox*, one he could not decipher.

Nick closed his eyes and tried to breathe normally. He was way too emotionally involved to think clearly. He began to pray. "I just want to be fair and *judicious* with this money. Just give me a sign."

His mom knocked on the door.

"Honey, it's about time to go to the church…How are you feeling?"

"I'm doing OK, Mom."

"Well, do you feel like going?" she asked.

"Yeah, just give me a few minutes."

Nick took a deep breath. He felt beat up by emotions. He grabbed his backpack with all the money in it and reluctantly put it on his back. "I just want this whole thing to be over with," he said to himself.

Nick and Sarah Franklin arrived at Second Bloom-

Precept	(**pree**-sept) – N – a command or principle intended especially as a general rule of action
Paradox	(**par**-uh-doks) – N – one (as a person, situation, or action) having seemingly contradictory qualities or phases
Judicious	(joo-**dish**-uhs) – ADJ – having, exercising, or characterized by sound judgment

ington Church at 11:00 p.m. The sanctuary was filled with parishioners on their knees in prayer. The room was quiet. Only the sniffles of tears and the sounds of whispers could be heard. On the stage sat Reverend Grey, who looked deep in thought. In front of the altar sat a coffer with a cross on the front. Nick and Sarah took their usual seats. Sarah bowed her head in prayer, and Nick mimicked her action. Reverend Grey began to speak.

"My brothers and sisters," he said. "Let me quickly give you a *terse* summary of why we are all here tonight. Our brother Tom Finley is ailing. He has been diagnosed with brain cancer. The doctors say that he has little time left. First and foremost, we are here to pray. But we are also here to help. Brothers and sisters, our brother Tom has a great need. He will be facing some hefty medical bills if he can get this surgery. We must not skip this opportunity to help him. Brothers and sisters, we have the chance to help him because of Nick…I mean…because we caught it in just the nick of time."

Nick took that little blunder as a *divine* sign from God telling him what to do.

"Rise up," the reverend continued, "and bring this brother your gifts. This is what we're all about, helping one another and blessing each other. Come to the front and place your gifts before the altar."

One by one, churchgoers stood from their seats and walked to the front. Nick felt pulled by the *onerous* burden to rise to the front, but he remained motionless. He'd been given the sign, but obedience was still too hard to handle.

Terse	(turs) – ADJ – devoid of superfluity; short
Divine	(dih-**vahyn**) – ADJ – heavenly; proceeding from God
Onerous	(**on**-er-uhs) – ADJ – burdensome, oppressive, or troublesome; causing hardship

By giving up this money, he would *forsake* any and all hopes he had of following his plans to become "somebody" at his school. He would be rewarding the family of the person who maliciously destroyed the only important possession he had ever had. He would be giving up every claim to independence that he had always dreamed about. He would doom himself to a life of being a victim of cruel schemes and mean jokes. Ryan would receive this blessing without ever having to pay *penance* for his sins.

With all these thoughts swirling in his head, Nick walked to the altar. He placed his backpack on the ground, and secretively pulled out the bundle of cash. He held it before the sparsely filled coffer, and gave it one last loving look. He dropped it in.

He was finally free.

Forsake	(fawr-**seyk**) – V – to give up; to renounce
Penance	(**pen**-uhns) – N – a punishment undergone in token of penitence for sin

WORD REVIEW

Abnegate
Depredate
Divine
Doldrums
Dullard
Forsake
Ghastly
Impasse
Judicious

Lament
Modus Operandi
Onerous
Pacify
Paradox
Pathos
Penance
Precarious
Precept

Rancor
Recondite
Tantamount
Terse
Turbid
Unsung
Wanton

17

C eleste arrived the next day at the scene of the crime in order to create a *postmortem* news report of the tragic fire. A pile of rubble was still smoldering and smoking in the center of the property. The fire inspector, Charles Sweeney, was already there. He was a man of diminutive stature. He wore a brown trench coat and a gray fedora and appeared to be the *quintessential* inspector.

Sweeney stood in the yard. He methodically poked his metallic cane through the residual ashes from the fire, *conscientiously* looking for clues. He had the habit of wiggling his nose and thick brown mustache each time he found something interesting, but so far, he had uncovered nothing. The fire had completely destroyed the house and its contents—and with it probably most of the evidence. Sweeney was deep in thought when Celeste approached him.

"Excuse me, sir." He jumped in surprise. "What have you discovered so far?" she asked him.

Postmortem	(pohst-**mawr**-tuhm) - ADJ – occurring after death; after the conclusion of an event
Quintessential	(kwin-tuh-**sen**-shuhl) – ADJ – the most typical example or representative
Conscientiously	(kon-shee-**en**-shuhs-lee) – ADV – meticulously; carefully

"Nothing but a whole lot of **desultory** evidence that won't help with solving this crime," he said. "Some trash, some debris—everything was completely destroyed, so it's hard to tell. I do know from the marks in the grass that this was a gasoline fire, and as such, it had to be intentional."

"Who would do such a thing?"

"There's no telling just yet. Maybe a form of revenge."

"May I take a look?"

"Sure, I'm just about to wrap it up. You would be lucky to find any more clues. Be careful—what's left of the house isn't sturdy."

"Thanks," Celeste replied and began her search. She pulled yellow rubber kitchen gloves from her bag and put them on. Then she started digging, her eyes on the lookout for anything foreign or unusual.

In the distance, Police Chief Briggs arrived at the scene. He was met by Sweeney, and they began to discuss the case. Sweeney was disappointed to have found only *tangential* evidence, nothing of substance.

Suddenly, Celeste caught a glimpse of something metallic buried in the dirt. She reached over and dug it up. It looked very peculiar and suspicious. It was the nozzle of a water hose cut off. "I found something!" she shouted, waving her hands above her head to attract the attention of the law officers. Sweeney ran over to her in excitement. Briggs followed him.

"Look," Celeste said as she held out the nozzle. Sweeney looked at it in surprise.

Desultory	(**des**-uhl-tohr-ee) – ADJ – not connected with the main subject
Tangential	(tan-**jen**-shuhl) – ADJ – having little relevance

"This is it!" he said. "My **nascent** suspicion is confirmed! The gas was siphoned from a car. There was so much gas used, I knew it had to originate from a tank bigger than just a gas can. This has the modus operandi of the Fascist Freedom Militia group...How exciting! One of these signature fires in our very own town."

"I'll put a call out for their capture right away," Briggs said. He went to the radio in his car and sent out a warning.

"Young lady," Sweeney said. "You have a great supply of **acumen** in your investigative abilities. You were blessed with brains along with beauty."

"If you want to credit me as a good investigative journalist in the city newspaper, I would consider it a gracious thank you," Celeste said.

"That I can do," he told her.

Sarah and Nick Franklin arrived at the property at that moment. They got out of their car and looked at the wreckage.

Nick was tired. He had spent the entire night deciding whether or not to give Ryan up to the cops. But he had come to the conclusion early in the morning that Ryan needed to be with his dad in his time of need. Their family did not need the extra stress of an arson investigation.

Nick had also realized a lot about himself. He realized that he had been given a clean slate, a blessing in disguise. He was completely free from everything that had been holding him back. His refuge was destroyed,

---

Nascent	(**nas**-uhnt) – ADJ – having recently come into existence; developing
Acumen	(**ak**-yuh-muhn) – N – keenness and depth of perception, discernment, or discrimination especially in practical matters

but he was OK. He didn't need it any more. He was filled with a strong sense of independence. He didn't need those material things to give him comfort; he was strong on his own!

He also decided to tell his mom the whole story. When she woke up in the morning, Nick told her all about the money and what he had done with it. At first, she was a little upset that he hadn't told her sooner, but she was so very proud of the wonderful decisions that he had made.

They walked up to the property and placed a "for sale" sign in the front yard. Nick hammered it into the ground with some tools from the back of their car. He and his mom had decided to sell the property, and with the money that was raised, put it in a college fund for Nick. Surprisingly, Nick was filled with contentment. Oh, he was tired all right, but deep inside, beyond the exhaustion, he was at peace.

As they approached the place where the house stood, Nick was met by Celeste. She gave him a hug. "I'm so sorry about this, Nick," she said. "They're going to catch the guys who did this."

"It's OK," he responded. "It will all be OK."

Nick walked over the remaining fragments of his penthouse. He couldn't help but feel a sense of remorse. It was all gone. Nick looked up to his mom, and in an almost excited voice described what the interior looked like.

"Here," he said as he *circumscribed* the room outline with his foot. "This was the game room. I had painted it green." Nick ran to the next room. "Here was the bedroom with a really nice bed. It felt like heaven when you lay down

---

Circumscribe   (**sur**-kuhm-skrahyb) – V – to encircle; to enclose
within limits

on it. You would have loved it. Here was the library. I'm glad I had read all those old books a million times. I need to get some new ones anyway..." Nick continued showing his mom the fortress that he had made. They pleasantly relished the existence of what the penthouse had been and pretended to forget its *immutable* fate. As Nick talked, Sarah was overcome with pride. She stopped him and hugged him tight. "I love you, son," she said. "You are going to do great things in this world."

Celeste had been watching this interaction with *innocuous* curiosity rather than her normal hard-hitting, investigative observation style. At that point, however, she felt the need to leave them in peace. Celeste walked over to the car she had borrowed from her dad and drove away. With the mystery of the fire culprits solved, she was off to ponder the one that had been haunting her all summer. *Who was the Summer Santa?*

It had to be somebody she knew. Maybe even someone she saw everyday. In order for him to find out about all the problems in town, he would have to live there and walk around.

Celeste parked her car in front of Red's Diner. She walked in and sat at her usual table. On pensive mornings, like this one, she loved having a cup of coffee and a plate of scrambled eggs. This was her "thought meal." Bea, Red's head waitress, came over to Celeste's table.

"Would you like the usual?" she asked.

"Yes, Bea," Celeste responded. "And can I get the paper, too?"

Immutable	(i-**myoo**-tuh-buhl) – ADJ – not capable of or susceptible to change
Innocuous	(i-**nok**-yoo-uhs) – ADJ – not likely to give offense or to arouse strong feelings or hostility

"Sure thing, sweetie."

Celeste *delved* into the clues she had to try to solve the Summer Santa mystery. The mayor said he was male. He had close access to her dad. He had to be present in town most of the summer. He had access to a large source of money.

There was some element missing, but she did not know what.

Bea brought out Celeste's order and set the paper on the table. Celeste poured cream and sugar into her coffee cup. She wished she could drink it black, like she knew all the top reporters in the world did. She also knew that someday she would be able to do it, but for now, she had to acclimate herself to it slowly. She wasn't a serious journalist yet, so she could allow herself some slack.

She always ate scrambled eggs because of their protein. Nothing helps the mind work better than protein. Celeste chewed her eggs in small bites. She began to read her paper. The top story was the fire. She perused the story, and then went on to read the rest of the publication.

The Bloomington Times was no newspaper of merit. The inside was generally filled with garbage, featuring mostly *pedantic* stories about city restructuring or *vapid* stories about social happenings. Celeste had been published in it quite a few times. She was the paper's number one contact for news regarding Bloomington High School. Never, though, had she been on the front page. Never before had any non-staff writer been on the front page. If Celeste could make it, she would frame the

Delve	(delv) – V – to examine a subject in detail
Pedantic	(puh-**dan**-tik) – ADJ – narrow, and often ostentatiously learned
Vapid	(**vap**-id) – ADJ – lacking liveliness, tang, briskness, or force

newspaper. Her dad would hang it on his wall. It would be an eternal honor.

She was more determined than ever to discover the identity of the Summer Santa.

A knock came at the window opposite Celeste. She looked up from her musings and saw Misty smiling and waving at her. Larry and Tracie followed closely behind. Celeste smiled back at them and walked over to the window.

"Sing sun full pap," Misty's *inchoate* words came muffled through the thick glass. Celeste gave a shrug and shook her head.

"Sing sun full pap," Misty repeated excitedly.

Celeste mouthed to her, "I can't hear you!"

The three friends ran around the building and came through the front exceedingly happy. "Something wonderful has happened!" Misty screamed.

"What?" asked Celeste anxiously.

"At last night's vigil for Ryan's dad, they raised the money for his surgery!"

"That's wonderful!" Celeste replied, thrilled at the news.

Misty hugged her and picked her up off the ground. "There's a very good chance that this *deleterious* condition can be cured."

"I'm so happy about this," Celeste said. "How's Ryan doing?"

"Ryan is gone. He and his dad left for Chicago early this morning."

Inchoate	(in-**koh**-it) – ADJ – imperfectly formed or formulated
Deleterious	(del-i-**teer**-ee-uhs) – ADJ – harmful often in a subtle way

"What exactly is the procedure that he's going to have?"

Misty thought for a second. "Well, for a few days the doctors are going to *macerate* the cancer with chemotherapy. After it's weakened a little, they intend to do an intensive surgery to cut it out of his brain. It's really scary, but I know it's going to work."

"Wow. I really hope it does."

"I have good news too!" Tracie jumped in. "On my porch, sitting with a little typed-up note, was the Golden Watermelon!"

"Really?"

"Yeah, the note said, 'You deserve this!' I have no idea how it got there, but I don't think Trudy Jones would be benevolent enough to hand this over."

"I bet it's that Santa guy," Larry added. "Who else would go out of his way to do something like that? He's been helping people out all over town."

"Wow, that's great," Celeste responded.

"Celeste, you need to figure out who this is, so we can thank him!" Tracie shouted.

"I don't think that's the point," Larry replied adamantly. "Maybe it's less about the gifts, and more about being nicer to people."

"Either way," Celeste stated, "I'm going to figure this out."

"Well, we need to go," said Misty. "We need to spread the news about Ryan's dad. I'll see you later."

"OK, bye, guys!"

Misty and her two friends ran out the door and sped down the street. Celeste returned to her chair. She was in

---

Macerate (**mas**-uh-reyt) – V – to cause to waste away by or as if by excessive fasting awe of the amazing gift that Mr. Finley had been given. She wondered if someone other than just the parishioners of Second Bloomington Church was involved. Someone like Summer Santa. One hundred thousand dollars was a lot of money—probably not anything the congregation could put together on their own.

The only person who knew the truth was her father. After Celeste finished eating, she planned to make an unexpected visit to her dad's office to see if she could find out anything.

WORD REVIEW

Acumen	Immutable	Postmortem
Circumscribe	Inchoate	Quintessential
Conscientiously	Innocuous	Tangential
Deleterious	Macerate	Vapid
Delve	Nascent	
Desultory	Pedantic	

18

"This is a personal *aspersion* against my client's good name," James Bering said to Pete the plumber, pointing at his advertisement in the paper. "My client has every right to file suit against you. Publishing such filth is *illicit* and unlawful behavior."

"It wasn't directed at him," Pete replied defensively. "This is ridiculous."

"There is only one other plumber in Bloomington, and he's been established here for years. There's no one else it could refer to."

"It's very vague! It could be anyone."

Bering didn't buy it. "If nothing else, these words are deceptive and *illusory*. There is no way to prove superiority, but you state it like it's fact."

"I *am* a better plumber, and I am *not* afraid to admit it."

"Look, my client is prepared to file a suit that will effectively liquidate your net worth. As a lawyer, I know I will win this case. He's willing to offer a bargain. He'll drop all charges if you relocate your business."

"Are you kidding?" Pete replied.

Aspersion	(uh-**spur**-zhuhn) – N – a false or misleading charge meant to harm someone's reputation
Illicit	(i-**lis**-it) – ADJ – not permitted
Illusory	(i-**loo**-suh-ree) – ADJ – like an illusion; deceptive

Bering wasn't kidding. "You haven't settled here yet. It will be a whole lot easier than going through court. Besides, this is a small town. Everyone will talk about it and it's very likely that the general populace will start a blackball."

"Fine. I'll think about your proposal," Pete said, knowing there wasn't much else he could do.

A knock came at the door. Celeste opened it and walked in without waiting for a response.

"Oh, sorry," she said when she found her dad preoccupied. She started to pull back out of the office.

"Wait, sweetheart," Bering said. "Our business is over."

Pete gave Celeste a polite smile. He sighed, got out of his chair, and stretched.

"Good day to you, ma'am; good day, Mr. Bering," Pete said as he walked out of the room.

"What were you doing with Pete the plumber?" Celeste asked.

"Nothing much," her dad replied. "My business is through with him. He's going to be leaving town soon."

Mr. Bering smiled at his daughter, curious to discover what had brought her to the office.

"Mr. Finley's surgery," she said. "Was that the work of the Summer Santa?"

"That transaction I did not handle," he said. "If it was Santa, he did it personally. It could just be a miracle, you know."

"Or a saint *performing* a miracle."

"I guess you're right," he responded.

"So, is Summer Santa done? I mean, is he finished giving money?"

"Is summer almost over? Because they wouldn't call him 'Summer Santa' if he gave money away in the winter."

"Would you consider him a *potentate*, someone powerful like you or the mayor?"

"If by 'potentate' you mean city official, I think I'm safe to say that he's not."

"Then he's just an average guy, part of the *proletariat*."

"Yes, as average as can be," he replied. "Any more questions?"

"No, I think you've told me more than enough."

Celeste turned away from her dad, smiling.

"I'll see you later," she called back to him triumphantly. Celeste ran all the way home. She ran upstairs to her room. Underneath her bed she kept an old typewriter, her lucky professional tool. It was missing the "q" key and had an ink ribbon with a *doddering*, feeble control, but she loved it. She knew that someday she would write an article with it that would win a Pulitzer Prize. She began to type.

Celeste had surmised that there was only one person in town whom her dad had contact with that she did not know their business. Coincidentally (or not), he was also someone who seemed to be around town during times of tremendous gift-giving. There was also no way of knowing how much money he had. And, as icing on the cake, he was planning to leave town at the end of the summer.

She typed quickly, her fingers flying. She put her entire conspiracy theory on paper. When she finished, she pulled out the thick yellow sheet she had typed on, thoroughly satisfied. This was the work of a real investi-

Potentate	(**poht**-n-teyt) – N – one who wields great power or sway
Proletariat	(proh-li-**tair**-ee-uht) – N – the lowest social or economic class of a community
Doddering	(**dod**-er-ing) – ADJ – feeble; senile

gative journalist. It was her greatest piece to date, full of suspense and intrigue. She read it over several times, and each time she thought it got better.

Celeste ran downstairs to find her dad sitting in his usual spot. She gave him the article, in which he was quoted several times. Mr. Bering perused the article and began to laugh hysterically.

"Well you did learn one thing," he said. "I'm a good source to quote."

"I'm sending it to the paper today," she responded, offended.

"Well that is some *effrontery*," he said, "sending it in as fact without any confirmation. I would hate for you to have to *abjure* your story if evidence comes out to prove it false."

"Am I not right?" she asked. "Because I'm pretty sure that I am."

"You'll find no one to contradict you. I would suggest interviewing me, but that's not needed. I'm already quoted."

"You *are* a good source, Daddy."

"I just have one question for you. How did you figure it out? Where did you find the *germane* evidence among all the irrelevant clues? Of course I only want to know because I want to see where I messed up. How maybe next time I could keep the secret better."

"Dad, you are so obvious all the time—I can see right through you."

Effrontery	(i-**fruhn**-tuh-ree) – N – shameless boldness
Abjure	(ab-**joor**)- V – to renounce or retract formally
Germane	(jer-**meyn**) – ADJ – being at once relevant and appropriate

"But seriously, how did you know?"

"A reporter never tells her secrets," she responded, "unlike city lawyers."

"Well, sweetie," he said, "I'm excited for you. This will be a great opportunity for you, if the Bloomington Times accepts it."

"They're *going* to accept it. It's the best piece of writing they've encountered in the last fifty years. It's interesting, too."

"We Berings are nothing, if not talented…You have my *imprimatur* to send it to print. I think it will make a lot of people happy, especially the mayor."

"Thanks, Daddy. I'm going to drive down to the paper office right away. Stop the presses—we've got a killer story coming."

Celeste took her manuscript and bundled it up in a folder. She kissed her dad, and then took his car keys off the table.

"I'm going to borrow your car—I hope that's OK." She ran outside and drove off.

Bering sat in his chair utterly dumbfounded. How Celeste came to such an off-the-wall conclusion, he had no idea. Fortunately, by the time it was printed, the person in question would be long out of town. It was a good thing, too. This story would make him a celebrity.

Bering was simply glad the whole thing was over. Everyone would forget and hopefully never find out about the real perpetrator, whom he truly wanted to protect.

Nick Franklin was a good kid, and if this town ever found out about his secret identity, he would be confronted with more problems than any child should have to bear.

Imprimatur　　(im-pri-**mey**-ter) – N – approval of a publication under circumstances of official censorship

WORD REVIEW

Abjure	Germane	Potentate
Aspersion	Illicit	Proletariat
Doddering	Illusory	
Effrontery	Imprimatur	

19

"Summer Santa Revealed!" Celeste read the front page of the paper. She was once again marveling at her conspicuous byline at the top.

"Let me read it to you," she said into the phone receiver. Ryan had called her from Chicago. She took the framed paper off the wall and began to read.

> "This summer there has been a mystery haunting Bloomington. Many unusual occurrences have appeared with no explanation. Unlike other towns with murders, rapes, and robberies, we citizens have been mysteriously struck by a rash of anonymous gift-giving. The perpetrator of such actions was not content with singly committing this act, but became a serial giver, one who affected most townspeople in one way or another. The acts became so egregious that Mayor Hill was forced to give him a title: 'Summer Santa.' People theorized on his identity. Perhaps he was rich and powerful. Perhaps he was a city official. Perhaps he was someone in our own family. The fact that he was a saint was the only conclusion agreed upon.

Summer Santa is not someone with great power and influence, but merely a **layman**, an ordinary guy with the extraordinary gift of generosity. There is good reason to believe that Peter Trabecki, the plumber, is the true identity of Summer Santa. He, along with Mayor Hill and James Bering, formed a **cabal** of secret generosity. Hill and Bering acted as **ancillary** help to the gift-giving spree. The three worked together to find problems in the community, and repair them with the money that Peter so willingly donated.

When his work was done, Trabecki exited Bloomington as quietly as he had arrived, never letting on his secret identity. He had only intended a summer of giving, and as the summer departed, so did he. 'Would he be called Summer Santa if he gave money in the winter?' said Bering, a close friend and associate of Trabecki.

If Trabecki were still in town today, I for one would like to shake his hand."

Celeste replaced the frame back on the wall.

"How do you like it?" she asked Ryan on the phone.

"That's interesting," Ryan responded on the other line.

"You've missed a lot of things since you've been away."

"Feel free to catch me up," he told her.

"Well Police Chief Briggs caught one of the

Layman	(**ley**-muhn) – N – a person who does not belong to a particular profession or who is not expert in some field
Cabal	(kuh-**bal**) – N – the artifices and intrigues of a group of persons secretly united in a plot
Ancillary	(an-**sil**-uh-ree) – ADJ – subordinate; subsidiary

members of the Fascist Freedom group. He, of course, denies all allegations of the fire, but they always do. He's being held for more serious crimes anyway."

"Really? That's awesome!" Ryan said excitedly. "I'm glad they caught the guy responsible for that **unconscionable** crime."

"Oh, yeah…and Sandra has a boyfriend. His name's Walter. He's kind of cute, but way too sappy."

"That's her type," he responded.

"You do realize that school starts tomorrow, right? Are you going to be back in time?"

"That's why I called you. My dad and I are catching a plane this evening from Chicago O'Hare."

"How's your dad doing?"

"His strength has been **enervated**, so he's really tired, but the doctors expect him to make a full recovery… Anyway, do you remember that favor you owe me?"

"Yes," Celeste said.

"Is there any way you could go to our apartment today and clean it up a little? I really want Dad to come home to a clean house."

"You know, I would love to do that," she **acceded**.

"Thanks. You're a doll."

"I know," Celeste responded.

"Well, I got to run. I'll see you at school tomorrow."

"Until tomorrow."

Celeste hung up the phone, but left the receiver in her hand. She immediately dialed Sandra's number.

Unconscionable	(uhn-**kon**-shuh-nuh-buhl) – ADJ – shockingly unfair or unjust
Enervate	(**en**-er-vey-t) – V – to reduce (the mental or moral vigor of)
Accede	(ak-**seed**) – V – to express approval or give consent

"Sandra?"

"Why, hello Celeste. How are you this afternoon?" she replied in a British accent.

"Have you done your good deed for today?"

"Hang it all! It must have slipped my mind."

"Then, boy, do I have an opportunity for you!"

"Oh, how rather exciting. Do tell."

"You see," Celeste said, picking up the accent, "Ryan had requested my service to aid in the sanitization of his apartment before his father returned to the country."

"So you want me to help you clean a house?" Sandra replied in her normal voice.

"It's for charity."

Sandra sighed. "Normally, I would *not* consider Ryan charity. However, on this occasion I will agree to your demands. Let me guess. You want me to pick you up?"

"You are smart and friendly. Walter has found quite a catch."

"I'll be over in a bit," Sandra said.

She arrived a few minutes later and Celeste got in the car.

"I hope you realize that you are robbing me of my last day of freedom," Sandra complained.

"You have nothing better to do," Celeste replied **impenitently**.

"Well, I'm missing my stories."

The two drove off on the road. They arrived at the apartment complex where Ryan lived. There was a fake rock beside the door, and Celeste picked it up and removed the key from inside. She unlocked the door. When it opened

---

Impenitently   (im-**pen**-i-tuhnt-lee) – ADV – not repentantly

both girls were filled with disgust. The place was a *squalid* wreck with dirty dishes, scattered clothes, and overflowing trashcans—a habitat typical of two bachelors.

"Why are we doing this again?" Sandra asked, overwhelmed.

"Because a sanitary environment is *conducive* to recovery."

"I don't even know where to start," Sandra exclaimed.

"How about the bathroom!" Celeste replied.

"If I had known that this trip *entailed* bathroom cleaning, I would *not* have come."

"Fine," Celeste said. "I'll do the bathroom. You start with the dishes."

Celeste went into the bathroom. There was absolutely no way to know when it was last cleaned. Clearly, it had been a very, very long time. The key decorating characteristic of the room was mold. The shower had black, brown, and what appeared to be purple mold spotted around it. The sink had some green mold and unique reddish mold around the fixtures. The toilet will not be described.

Celeste began cleaning. In the shower, she could scrape off a layer of gunk only to find another layer underneath. She sprayed cleaner over the entire bathroom, on everything porcelain, ceramic, or just plain dirty-looking. She washed, and scraped, and sprayed, and washed some more. Eventually the sight of white cleanness began to shine from her work.

Squalid	(**skwawl**-id) – ADJ – marked by filthiness and degradation from neglect or poverty
Conducive	(kuhn-**doo**-siv) – ADJ – tending to promote or assist
Entail	(en-**teyl**) – V – to involve; to include

Meanwhile, Sandra tackled the dishes. First she filled the sink with soapy water, and then placed the most challenging items in it to soak. She then explored the entire apartment in search of misplaced dish articles. She found them everywhere, so she had to make several trips back and forth. By the time she was done, her pile of dirty dishes had tripled in size. She became disappointed and approached the job with *lackluster* spirit. She pulled a plate from the soapy water. It appeared to have had Chinese food on it beforehand. She got out a scrub brush and scrubbed. The embedded crust would not budge. Her soapy soak had proved *inefficacious* against the stubborn caked-on food remainders. She got out a knife and began scraping the gunk with it. She made slow progress, but eventually she was able to clean it. With steady continuous effort, Sandra was able to complete the job.

As soon as Sandra finished the dishes, Celeste met her and said, "Let's tackle the living room." This was another daunting task. There was junk piled everywhere and no clear organization to the room. Sandra *furrowed* her brow in contemplation.

"What we could do," she said, "is make piles of different types of things. One pile for clothes, one for papers, and so forth. From there we can decide what to do with the piles."

"Sounds good," Celeste replied.

The two girls began piling. Sandra's idea proved to be very effective in the cleaning process. In no time, they had separated the room into neat little piles. They put

Lackluster	(**lak**-luhs-ter) – ADJ – lacking liveliness, vitality, spirit, or enthusiasm
Inefficacious	(in-ef-i-**key**-shuhs) – ADJ – lacking the power to produce a desired effect
Furrow	(**fuhr**-oh) – V – to make grooves, wrinkles, or lines in

everything away, and then took on the two bedrooms. They made the beds, organized the floor, and generally put the rooms in order.

After all this was done, they met back in the living room. Sandra surveyed their work. The apartment looked sanitary. Everything was in order and it appeared to finally have the woman's touch. Celeste hugged Sandra and thanked her for the help.

WORD REVIEW

Accede	Entail	Layman
Ancillary	Furrow	Squalid
Cabal	Impenitently	Unconscionable
Conducive	Inefficacious	
Enervate	Lackluster	

Nick woke up nervous. Another school year had come. He wanted to stay in bed.

He considered quitting. What could the last two years of high school possibly teach him? He was probably getting more life experience staying in bed than he would in the classrooms of Bloomington High. So he made a decision. He would simply never get out of bed. He could have a television brought in, and he could spend the rest of his days watching soap operas and talk shows. Maybe he could become a daytime TV critic for the local paper.

The *hoi polloi* around the world would be mildly curious about the boy who had not left his bed for thirty years. Someday, maybe after he had received a large cult following, he would make a triumphant return to the world. The fans would wait outside his house for days, hoping to see his face. When he finally emerged, he would be on the cover of *Time* or *People*.

His firm decision to stay in bed weakened to an *irresolute* wish when he realized that he needed to go to the bathroom. In the future, he could get a catheter, but he had no time to wait for one now. And yet…if he got up now,

---

Hoi Polloi	(**hoi** puh-**loi**) – N – the masses; common folk
Irresolute	(i-**rez**-uh-loot) – ADJ – uncertain how to act or proceed

it would be over. The beauty of never getting up would disappear. The *corollary* of taking the first step of going to the bathroom would be the logical next step of going to school.

Nick had two options: hold it or go to school. He weighed both soundly. His moral fiber held to his resolution of a bedside lifestyle, but his bladder was angrily drawing his attention to the bathroom. Eventually, with all scrupulous reservations aside, Nick got out of bed. He sat up, and then rotated toward the side. First he placed his right foot on the cold, cold floor. Then the second foot followed suit. Nick jerked them both back up, hesitant to make the move final. Then he again returned them to the ground.

He stood victorious. Only the one red-striped sock on his right foot had survived the night in place, so he limped off balance all the way to the restroom.

Nick's mom was busy preparing breakfast. It had always been her tradition to make a big deal out of the first day of school. For some reason, she believed stuffing her son full of food would somehow ensure he would have a good day. She had prepared pancakes, fruit salad, sausage, bacon, hash browns, and currently, she was working on scrambled eggs with cheese and ham. If nothing else went well that day for Nick, at least breakfast would be awesome.

Nick encountered his mom as she was *pummeling* the eggs with her whisk. He came to her and gave her a big hug.

"There's plenty of food. You better get started. We don't want you to be late for school."

Corollary	(**kor**- uh-ler-ee) – N – something that naturally follows
Pummel	(**puhm**-uhl) – V – to pound; to beat

"I'm not going to school," Nick told her.

"Well that's a shame. I would hate for all this food to go to waste," she responded.

"I didn't say I wasn't going to eat."

Nick grabbed a plate and began piling food on it. He sat down and commenced shoveling the feast into his mouth. Watching him chew was a grotesque sight.

"If you're not going to school," his mom said, "that puts me in a perplexing *quandary*."

"How so?"

"Now what will I do with this fifty dollar bill that I was going to give to my child before he went off to school? I can't give it to you any more. You don't qualify. I wonder if there are any homeless people looking for some change."

"OK, Mom," he responded. "I will go to school—today."

"I'm going to definitely need a week's promise to relinquish this $50."

"I will go to school all week."

"Here you go," she said as she handed him the bill.

"Thanks, Mom."

"I may not receive the *kudos* that you do when it comes to gift-giving, but I do what I can."

"But Mom, you're the best gift-giver I know."

She kissed him on the forehead and looked at him lovingly. "Now come on!" she said. "Hurry up."

Nick ate his food quickly, or at least as quickly as he could, taking into account the size of the meal. After he finished, he went to his room and got dressed. He had one outfit left that he had gotten from Gringos. He was

---

Quandary	(**kwon**-dree) – N – a state of perplexity or doubt
Kudos	(**koo**-dohs) – N – fame and renown resulting from an act or achievement

wearing it the day of the fire, so it hadn't been destroyed. He put it on.

It was the best he had ever looked for a first day of school. Sure, he still didn't have a car and, yes, he was wearing glasses, but at least he felt cool. He grabbed his backpack full of brand new schoolbooks and headed out to meet his mom at the front of the house. She was already waiting for him, keys in hand.

"You're going to have a great day," she told him.

* * *

The regular crew was waiting outside the front of the school. They all sat in front chatting until the very second the bell rang. Everyone there was part of the *elite* crowd; normal kids were forced to endure their condescending stares in order to enter the school building. Most people, the incredibly average ones, were completely ignored, except on bad hair days. But there were a few, the *dregs* of the social ladder, who always caught the negative attention of the group.

Nick was part of this specially selected group.

The first day of school was always the worst because they paid extra-close attention. They had to examine the freshmen, see if anyone had lost or gained weight, and single out new members. It was a great day to look good, and a terrible day to look bad.

Elite   (i-**leet**) – ADJ – a group of persons who by virtue of position or education exercise much power or influence

Dregs   (dregs) – N – the most undesirable parts

Celeste and Sandra had located themselves at the prime spot on a bench under a tree. If the social world were a solar system, their position was the sun, and all other positions rotated around it in inferiority.

"I wish Walter hadn't graduated already," Sandra said. "I can't bear being at school all day without him."

"You'll be just fine, Sandra. Besides, maybe one of the new football recruits will change your decision about high school boys."

"Walter and I have found true love. Why would I want to mess up perfection with…" Sandra stopped as she watched a big group of freshman boys walk by. "Well, I guess I should keep an open mind. It would be wrong to judge them before I met them."

Nick pulled up to the school. He kissed his mom and anxiously got out of the car. He began to walk to the doors self-consciously. Fear filled him. His emotional state was anything but *esoteric*—one good look and the popular kids would see right through him.

Nick walked swiftly, hoping that he would avoid attention, but on the first day it was impossible for him to be overlooked. He heard, "Hey, Nick," coming from the cruel side of the school's front yard. He hoped with all his might that maybe one of his chess club friends just happened to be standing in that direction and calling for him. Maybe it was a freshman or somebody who didn't know the social norms and rules of the school.

He looked in that direction, but nowhere could he see anyone so innocuous—only cool people. And they were all

---

Esoteric   (es-uh-**ter**-ik) – ADJ – understood by or meant for only the select few who have special knowledge or interest

looking at him. At that moment, he noticed Celeste. She was walking over to talk to him.

"Nick, you must not have recognized my voice," she said. "I was calling you."

"Yeah, sorry. I just didn't know who it was."

"Well, I just wanted to tell you that I think you look nice today," she said. "I don't think you're going to get made fun of wearing these clothes, I mean, unless you wear them everyday."

"Thanks, Celeste. I appreciate it."

"No problem," she said. Celeste went back and sat with her friends. Nick was shocked. He had never received such approving *panegyric* or any kind of compliment from the other side before. It felt good to be praised. He looked around and realized that nobody was staring at him anymore. He was no longer ostracized. All it took was a new outfit and a conversation with somebody cool. He was free. Finally, the torment was over.

Suddenly, the attention of the entire student body was directed to the road by a loud, blaring sound. A black Corvette pulled up. Ryan came out of the driver's side. He walked around the car and opened the door for Misty. Both of them looked like celebrities. As they approached the group, people screamed with excitement. "Ryan! You're back! How's your dad? We missed you!"

If school were a kingdom, Ryan would be king.

As everyone was distracted, Nick walked into the building. He went to his homeroom class and sat down. It was several minutes before the bell would ring, so the room was sparsely populated. There were only a few nerds here

---

Panegyric   (pan-i-**jir**-ik) – N – formal or elaborate praise

and there. When the bell rang, students came pouring in, one of whom was Ryan.

Nick wondered how Ryan would react to his presence, if maybe he would feel sorry for his actions, or maybe grateful for his dad's surgery. Maybe the whole summer ordeal would have changed his outlook on the world. Maybe he would be a kinder, nicer guy.

Ryan passed by Nick without acknowledgement. It appeared as if Nick's forgiving and generous gestures toward him would be *unrequited,* passing into history without even the slightest acknowledgement. Nick was totally fine with that. If he had been kind to Ryan in order to win his approval, he would have a sad life. No, Nick was not desperate for Ryan's approval anymore. He just rested his mind on the solid knowledge of his moral superiority.

Mr. Schlipp entered the classroom. Once again, he would be their homeroom teacher. He said that he liked their class so much that he wanted to stay in grade with them until they graduated. The entire class was less than thrilled. Some people threw spitballs at him. Others just showed their approval by drawing caricatures of him dying. Nick showed his love by not paying any attention.

Finally the bell rang. Nick went to his classes. Some of them, like physics and social science, he really enjoyed. Others, like physical education, he hated. Overall, though, it had been a really good first day.

During the *cusp* between fourth period and fifth, Nick was met by Ryan.

"Buddy," Ryan said. "I'm sorry about what happened to

Unrequited	(uhn-ri-**kwahy**-tid) – ADJ – not reciprocated or returned in kind
Cusp	(kuhsp) – N – a point of transition

your house and all. You're a nice guy. I just can't pretend to like you in class. It would hurt my reputation. I got you this cola because I want to apologize."

Something in Ryan's voice hinted of insincerity, and after a summer of learning about life, Nick was no longer *gullible* enough to trust his antagonist. He tried to back away, but before Nick could move, Ryan sprayed soda all over Nick's new clothes and began laughing hysterically.

Ryan was not just a king, he was a tyrannical *despot.*

"Sucker! Didn't you learn anything this summer?"

Suddenly, Larry emerged from the background and stood in between Ryan and Nick.

"Hey, man," Larry intervened. "That's not cool. He didn't do anything to you."

Out of nowhere, Tracie appeared as well. "Seriously, Ryan. Grow up. Be nicer to people."

They both scowled at Ryan, who stormed off angrily. Larry turned to Nick.

"Are you okay?"

Nick nodded in response, shocked to have someone stand up for him. Tracie gave him a sympathetic smile, and his two defenders walked away nonchalantly.

Nick looked at his soiled shirt and the *ambiguous* wet spot on his pants, and smiled.

Gullible	(**guhl**-uh-buhl) – ADJ – easily deceived
Despot	(**des**-pot) – N – person exercising power tyrannically
Ambiguous	(am-**big**-yoo-uhs) – ADJ – doubtful or uncertain especially from obscurity or indistinctness

WORD REVIEW

Ambiguous	Elite	Kudos
Corollary	Esoteric	Panegyric
Cusp	Gullible	Pummel
Despot	Hoi Polloi	Quandary
Dregs	Irresolute	Unrequited

GLOSSARY

Aberrant - uh-**ber**-uhnt) - ADJ - deviating from the usual or
   natural type - page 116 - chapter 13

Abjure - (ab-**joor**) - V - to renounce or retract formally -
   page 174 - chapter 18

Abnegate - (**ab**-ni-geyt) - V - surrender; relinquish -
   page 149 - chapter 16

Accede - (ak-**seed**) - V - to express approval or give consent -
   page 179 - chapter 19

Accolade - (ak-uh-**leyd**) - N - a mark of acknowledgment -
   page 83 - chapter 10

Accord - (uh-**kawrd**) - N - agreement - page 83 - chapter 10

Accost - (uh-**kos**-t) - V - to approach and to speak to, often
   purposefully - page 73 - chapter 9

Accouterments - (uh-**koo**-ter-muhnts) - N - equipment;
   trappings - page 13 - chapter 1

Acumen - (**ak**-yuh-muhn) - N - keeness and depth of
   perception, discernment, or discrimination
   especially in practical matters -
   page 163 - chapter 17

Acute - (uh-**kyoot**) - ADJ - sharp penetrating in intellect,
   insight, or perception - page 63 - chapter 8

Adulate - (**aj**-uh-leyt) - V - to flatter; praise - page 121 -
   chapter 13

Affront - (uh-**fruhnt**) - N - a deliberate offence - page 125 -
   chapter 14

Alacrity - (uh-**lak**-ri-tee) - N - cheerful readiness or
   willingness - page 11 - chapter 1

Allay - (uh-**ley**) - V - subdue or reduce in intensity or
   severity - page 137 - chapter 14

Altruistic - (al-troo-**is**-tik) - ADJ - unselfish with regards to
   the welfare of others; humanitarian - page 80 -
   chapter 9

Ambience - (**am**-bee-uhns) - N - a feeling or mood associated with a particular place, person, or thing (note: also ambiance) - page 118 - chapter 13

Ambiguous - (am-**big**-yoo-uhs) - ADJ - doubtful or uncertain especially from obscurity or indistinctness - page 192 - chapter 20

Amble - (**am**-buhl) - N - a leisurely walk - page 13 - chapter 1

Amenable - (uh-**men**-uh-buhl) - ADJ - disposed or ready to yield or submit - page 62 - chapter 8

Ameliorate - (uh-**meel**-yuh-reyt) - V - to make more tolerable; to make easier - page 14 - chapter 1

Ancillary - (an-**sil**-uh-ree) - ADJ - subordinate; subsidiary - page 178 - chapter 19

Antedate - (an-ti-**deyt**) - V - to precede; to come before - page 93 - chapter 11

Antipathy - (an-**tip**-uh-thee) - N - settled aversion or dislike - page 120 - chapter 13

Apex - (**ey**- peks) - N - the highest point - page 119 - chapter 13

Apotheosis - (uh- poth-ee-**oh**-sis) - N - the perfect example - page 118 - chapter 13

Apportion - (uh- **pohr**-shuhn) - V - to divide and share out according to a plan - page 78 - chapter 9

Askance - (uh-**skans**) - ADV - with suspicion, mistrust, or disapproaval - page 45 - chapter 6

Aspersion - (uh-**spur**-zhuhn) - N - a false or misleading charge meant to harm someone's reputation - page 171 - chapter 18

Augur - (**aw**-ger) - V - to foretell; to foresee - page 92 - chapter 11

Avow - (uh-**vou**) - V - to declare assuredly - page 68 - chapter 8

Beleaguer - (bi-**lee**-ger) - V - to trouble; to harass - page 88 - chapter 10

Belittle - (bih-**lit**-l) - V - to disparage; to make small - page 25 - chapter 3

Bemused - (bi-**myoozd**) - ADJ - confused - page 85 - chapter 10

Benighted - (bi-**nahy**-tid) - ADJ - existing in a state of intellectual darkness - page 71 - chapter 9

Besmirch - (bi-**smurch**) - V - to soil; tarnish: discolor; to detract from the luster - page 12 - chapter 1

Bilious - (**bil**-yuhs) - ADJ - peevish; testy; cross - page 56 - chapter 8

Bonhomie - (**bon**-uh-mee) - N - good-natured easy friendliness - page 64 - chapter 8

Boons - (boons) - N - timely benefits - page 95 - chapter 11

Boor - (boor) - N - a rude or insensitive person - page 88 - chapter 10

Bucolic - (byoo-**kol**-ik) - ADJ - typically rural - page 15 - chapter 1

Burgeoning - (**bur**-juhn-ing) - ADJ - growing and rapidly expanding - page 103 - chapter 11

Cabal - (kuh-**bal**) - N - the artifices and intrigues of a group of persons secretely united in a plot - page 178 - chapter 19

Canvass - (**kan**-vuhs) - V - to examine in detail - page 79 - chapter 9

Cardinal - (**kahr**-dn-l) - ADJ - of prime importance; primary - page 58 - chapter 8

Cascade - (kas-**keyd**) - N - something falling or rushing forth in quantity - page 112 - chapter 12

Charily - (**chair**-uh-lee) - ADV - cautiously; hesitantly - page 98 - chapter 11

Circumscribe - (**sur**-kuhm-skrahyb) - V - to encircle; to enclose within limits - page 164 - chapter 17

Clairvoyant - (klair-**voi**-uhnt) - ADJ - having the power of seeing objects beyond the natural range of vision - page 13 - chapter 1

Clandestine - (klan-**des**-tin) - ADJ - secret; private; concealed - page 60 - chapter 8

Clique - (klik) - N - a group that is snobbishly exclusive - page 57 - chapter 8

Closefisted - (**klohs**-fis-tid) - ADJ - stingy - page 40 - chapter 5

Coalesce - (koh-uh-**les**) - V - united into a whole - page 74 - chapter 9

Cogitate - (**koj**-i-teyt) - V - to meditate deeply or intently - page 85 - chapter 10

Collusion - (kuh-**loo**-zhuhn) - N - secret agreement or cooperation especially for an illegal or deceitful purpose - page 126 - chapter 14

Commodious - (kuh-**moh**-dee-uhs) - ADJ - comfortable or spacious - page 79 - chapter 9

Competence - (**kom**- pi-tuhns) - N - sufficiency of means for the necessities and conveniences of life; capability - page 129 - chapter 14

Condescendingly - (kon-duh-**sen**-ding-lee) - ADV - patronizingly; degradingly - page 136 - chapter 14

Conducive - (kuhn-**doo**-siv) - ADJ - tending to promote or assist - page 181 - chapter 19

Conscientiously - (kon-shee-**en**-shuhs-lee) - ADV - meticulously; carefully - page 161 - chapter 17

Contiguous - (kuhn-**tig**-yoo-uhs) - ADJ - near in sequence; touching or sharing a border - page 77 - chapter 9

Conundrum - (kuh-**nuhn**-druhm) - N - an intricate and difficult problem - page 80 - chapter 9

Conversant - (**kon**-ver-suhnt) - ADJ - having knowledge or experience - page 102 - chapter 11

Corollary - (**kor**-uh-ler-ee) - N - something that naturally follows - page 186 - chapter 20

Credulity - (kruh-**dyoo**-li-tee) - N - readiness or willingness to believe especially on slight or uncertain evidence - page 123 - chapter 13

Cupidity - (kyoo- **pid**-i-tee) - N - page strongpage desire - page 103 - chapter 11

Cusp - (kuhsp) - N - a point of transition - page 191 - chapter 20

Dearth - (durth) - N - scarcity or scanty supply; lack - page 33 - chapter 4

Degrade - (di-**greyd**) - V - to lower in grade, rank, or status - page 130 - chapter 14

Deign - (deyn) - V - to condesend in order to give or offer something - page 107 - chapter 12

Dejected - (di-**jek**-tid) - ADJ - cast down in spirits; depressed - page 80 - chapter 9

Deleterious - (del-i-**teer**-ee-uhs) - ADJ - harmful often in a subtle way - page 167 - chapter 17

Delphic - (**del**-fik) - ADJ - oracular; obscure; ambiguous - page 14 - chapter 1

Delve - (delv) - V - to examine a subject in detail - page 166 - chapter 17

Demeanor - (di-**mee**-ner) - N - conduct; behavior - page 45 - chapter 6

Demotic - (dih-**mot**-ik) - ADJ - popular; vernacular; of or pertaining to common speech - page 12 - chapter 1

Denizen - (**den**-uh-zuhn) - N - an inhabitant; resident - page 31 - chapter 4

Depredate - (**dep**-ri-deyt) - V - to plunder; ravage - page 153 - chapter 16

Deride - (di-**rahyd**) - V - to subject to bitter or contemptuous ridicule - page 67 - chapter 8

Desist - (di-**sist**) - V - to cease to proceed or act - page 95 - chapter 11

Despot - (**des**- pot) - N - person exercising power tyranni-
cally - page 192 - chapter 20

Desultory - (**des**-uhl-tohr-ee) - ADJ - not connected with the
main subject - page 162 - chapter 17

Dialectical - (dahy-uh-**lek**-ti-kuhl) - ADJ - coming to a
conclusion by merging two opposing views -
page 131 - chapter 14

Diaphanous - (dahy-**af**-uh-nuhs) - ADJ - characterized by
extreme delicacy of form; transparent - page 146 -
chapter 15

Dichotomy - (dahy-**kot**-uh-mee) - N - something with
seemingly contradictory qualities - page 94 -
chapter 11

Diffidence - (**diff**-i-duhns) - N - the state of being hesitant in
acting or speaking through lack of self- confidence -
page 101 - chapter 11

Dilapidated - (di-**lap**-i-deyt-ed) - ADJ - reduced to or fallen
into ruin or decay - page 38 - chapter 5

Dirge - (durj) - N - song or hymns of grief or lamentation -
page 63 - chapter 8

Discomfit - (dis-**kuhm**-fit) - V - to put into a state of
perplexity and embarrassment - page 136 -
chapter 14

Disconsolate - (dis-**kon**-suh-lit) - ADJ - without hope;
hopelessly unhappy - page 25 - chapter 3

Dissemble - (di-**sem**-buhl) - V - to conceal the real nature;
to put on an appearance of - page 23 - chapter 3

Diurnal - (dahy-**ur**-nl) - ADJ - of or pertaining to each day;
active by day (opposed to nocturnal) - page 33 -
chapter 4

Divine - (dih-**vahyn**) - ADJ - heavenly; proceeding from
God - page 158 - chapter 16

Doddering - (**dod**-er-ing) - ADJ - feeble; senile -
page 173 - chapter 18

Doggedly - (**dog**-id-lee) - ADV - persisently - page 39 - chapter 5

Doldrums - (**dohl**-druhmz) - N - a spell of listessness or despondency - page 155 - chapter 16

Domicile - (**dom**-uh-sahyl) - N - place of residence - page 17 - chapter 2

Dregs - (dregs) - N - the most undesirable parts - page 188 - chapter 20

Droll - (drohl) - ADJ - having a humourous, whimsical or odd quality - page 117 - chapter 13

Dulcet - (**duhl**-sit) - ADJ - pleasing to the ear - page 76 - chapter 9

Dullard - (**duhl**-erd) - N - a stupid or unimaginative person - page 152 - chapter 16

Effrontery - (i-**fruhn**-tuh-ree) - N - shameless boldness - page 174 - chapter 18

Egocentric - (ee-goh-**sen**-trik) - ADJ - limited in outlook or concern to ones own activities or needs - page 68 - chapter 8

Egregious - (i-**gree**-juhs) - ADJ - conspiciously bad - page 103 - chapter 11

Elite - (i-**leet**) - ADJ - a group of persons who by virtue of position or educatoin exercise much power of influence - page 188 - chapter 20

Elusive - (i-**loo**-siv) - ADJ - tending to evade grasp or pursuit - page 93 - chapter 11

Emaciation - (i-mey-see-**ey**-shuhn) - N - loss of flesh so as to become very thin - page 99 - chapter 11

Eminent - (**em**-uh-nuhnt) - ADJ - high in station, rank, or repute - page 30 - chapter 4

Emissary - (**em**-uh-ser-ee) - N - an agent sent on a mission or errand - page 55 - chapter 8

Emollient - (i-**mol**-yuhnt) - ADJ - having the power of softening or relaxing - page 44 - chapter 6

Empower - (em- **pou**-er) - V - to promote the self-actualization or influence of something or someone - page 101 - chapter 11

Encroach - (en-**krohch**) - V - to advance beyond the usual or proper limits - page 143 - chapter 15

Endogenous - (en-**doj**-uh-nuhs) - ADJ - derived internally; proceeding from within - page 24 - chapter 3

Enervate - (**en**-er-vey-t) - V - to reduce (the mental or moral vigor of) - page 179 - chapter 19

Enigma - (uh-**nig**-muh) - N - something hard to understand or explain - page 84 - chapter 10

Ensconce - (en-**skons**) - V - to settle snugly or securely - page 15 - chapter 1

Entail - (en-**teyl**) - V - to involve; to include - page 181 - chapter 19

Envision - (en-**vizh**-uhn) - V - to picture mentally, generally of the future - page 37 - chapter 5

Equivocal - (i-**kwiv**-uh-kuhl) - ADJ - of uncertain nature or classification - page 110 - chapter 12

Erstwhile - (**urst**-wahyl) - ADJ - former; previous - page 132 - chapter 14

Erudition - (er-yoo-**dish**-uhn) - N - acquired knowledge; scholarship - page 32 - chapter 4

Esoteric - (es-uh-**ter**-ik) - ADJ - understood by or meant for only the select few who have special knowledge or interest - page 189 - chapter 20

Estimable - (**es**-tuh-muh-buhl) - ADJ - worthy of esteem - page 75 - chapter 9

Euphemism - (**yoo**-fuh-miz-hum) - N - the substitution of an agreeable or inoffensive expression for one that may offend or suggest something unpleasant - page 137 - chapter 14

Evoke - (i-**vohk**) - V - to call forth or up - page 117 - chapter 13

Exacerbate - (ig-**zas**-er-beyt) - V - to make more violent, bitter, or severe - page 144 - chapter 15

Exploit - (**ek**-sploy-t) - V - to use selfishly for one's own ends - page 52 - chapter 7

Expropriate - (eks- **proh**- pree-yet) - V - to deprive of possesion or proprietary rights - page 146 - chapter 15

Extirpate - (**ek**-ster- pate) - V - to destroy completely - page 108 - chapter 12

Extol - (ik-**stohl**) - V - to praise highly - page 71 - chapter 9

Extraneous - (ik-**strey**-nee-uhs) - ADJ - not essential or vital - page 115 - chapter 13

Exultant - (ig-**zuhl**-tnt) - ADJ - highly elated; triumphant - page 43 - chapter 6

Facet - (**fas**-it) - N - any of the definable aspects that make up a subject or an object - page 138 - chapter 14

Fathom - (**fath**-uhm) - V - to penetrate and come to understand - page 132 - chapter 14

Feign - (feyn) - V - to pretend; to represent fictitiously - page 47 - chapter 6

Flay - (fley) - V - to criticize or reprove with scathing severity - page 59 - chapter 8

Forsake - (fawr-**seyk**) - V - to give up; to renounce - page 159 - chapter 16

Furrow - (**fuhr**-oh) - V - to make grooves, wrinkles, or lines in - page 182 - chapter 19

Gainsay - (**geyn**-say) - V - to declare to be untrue or invailid - page 125 - chapter 14

Germane - (jer-**meyn**) - ADJ - being at once relevant and appropriate - page 174 - chapter 18

Ghastly - (**gast**-lee) - ADJ - terrifyingly horrible to the senses - page 154 - chapter 16

Glibly - (**glib**-lee) - ADV - marked by ease and informality - page 96 - chapter 11

Glut - (gluht) - N - a full supply - page 30 - chapter 4

Gullible - (**guhl**-uh-buhl) - ADJ - easily deceived - page 192 - chapter 20

Harry - (**har**-ee) - V - to harass; to worry or annoy - page 134 - chapter 14

Hassock - (**has**-uhk) - N - a thick cushion used as a footstool or for kneeling - page 25 - chapter 3

Hedonistic - (**heed**-n-ist-ik) - ADJ - of the doctrine that pleasure or happiness is the sole or chief good in life - page 86 - chapter 10

Herald - (**her**-uhld) - V/N - to signal the approach of something, often with enthusiasm; one that conveys news or proclaims - page 91 - chapter 11

Heterodox - (**her**-er-uh-doks) - ADJ - contrary to an acknowledged standard, a tradional form, or an established religion - page 131 - chapter 14

Hoi Polloi - (**hoi** puh-**loi**) - N - the masses; common folk - page 185 - chapter 20

Ignominy - (ig-**nom**-uh-nee) - N - deep personal humiliation and disgrace - page 126 - chapter 14

Illicit - (i-**lis**-it) - ADJ - not permitted - page 171 - chapter 18

Illusory - (i-**loo**-suh-ree) - ADJ - like an illusion; deceptive - page 171 - chapter 18

Imbecility - (im-buh-**sil**-i-tee) - N - feebleness of mind; silliness or absurdity - page 34 - chapter 4

Immutable - (i-**myoo**-tuh-buhl) - ADJ - not capable of or susceptible to change - page 165 - chapter 17

Impasse - (im- **pas**) - N - a predicament affording no obvious escape - page 150 - chapter 16

Impeccable - (im- **pek**-uh-buhl) - ADJ - free from fault or blame; perfect - page 110 - chapter 12

Impenitently - (im- **pen**-i-tuhnt-lee) - ADV - not repentantly - page 180 - chapter 19

Imperative - (im- **per**-uh-tiv) - ADJ - necessary; not to be avoided - page 115 - chapter 13

Imprimatur - (im- pri-**mey**-ter) - N - approval of a publication under circumstances of official censorship - page 175 - chapter 18

Impudence - (**im**- pyuh-duhns) - N - bold insolence - page 63 - chapter 8

Inanely - (i-**neyn**-lee) - ADV - lacking significance, meaning, or point - page 118 - chapter 13

Inchoate - (in-**koh**-it) - ADJ - imperfectly formed or formulated - page 167 - chapter 17

Incipient - (in-**sip**-ee-uhnt) - ADJ - beginning to come into being or to become apparent - page 144 - chapter 15

Incongruous - (in-**kong**-groo-uhs) - ADJ - inconsistent - page 94 - chapter 11

Indefatigable - (in-di-**fat**-i-guh-buhl) - ADJ - incapable of being tired out; not yielding to fatigue - page 61 - chapter 8

Indolence - (**in**-dl-uhns) - N - the state of desiring to avoid exertion; laziness - page 31 - chapter 4

Inefficacious - (in-ef-i-**key**-shuhs) - ADJ - lacking the power to produce a desired effect - page 182 - chapter 19

Ingenue - (**an**-zhuh-noo) - N - a naïve and unworldly girl, especially in acting - page 59 - chapter 8

Innocuous - (i-**nok**-yoo-uhs) - ADJ - not likely to give offense or to arouse strong feelings or hostility - page165 - chapter 17

Inordinate - (in-**awr**-dn-it) - ADJ - excessive; uncontrolled - page 33 - chapter 4

Insufferably - (in-**suhf**-er-uh-buhlee) - ADV - intolerably; unbearingly - page 74 - chapter 9

Integral - (**in**-ti-gruhl) - ADJ - essential to completeness - page 75 - chapter 9

Interminable - (in-**tur**-muh-nuh-buhl) - ADJ - having or seeming to have no end - page 134 - chapter 14

Intransigently - (in-**tran**-si-juhnt-lee) - ADV - characterized by refusal to comprimise or to abandon an extreme position or attitude - page 129 - chapter 14

Inure - (in-**yoor**) - V - to toughen or harden; to become accustomed - page 33 - chapter 4

Inviolate - (in-**vahy**-uh-lit) - ADJ - not violated or profanned; pure - page 87 - chapter 10

Irascible - (i-**ras**-uh-buhl) - ADJ - marked by hot temper and easily provoked anger - page 133 - chapter 14

Irresolute - (i-**rez**-uh-loot) - ADJ - uncertain how to act or proceed - page 185 - chapter 20

Irrevocable - (i-**rev**-uh-kuh-buhl) - ADJ - not possible to revoke; unalterable - page 143 - chapter 15

Jostle - (**jos**-uhl) - V - make one's way by pushing and shoving - page 98 - chapter 11

Judicious - (joo-**dish**-uhs) - ADJ - having, exercising, or characterized by sound judgment - page 157 - chapter 16

Jurisprudence - (joor-is- **prood**-ns) - N - the science or philosophy of law - page 21 - chapter 3

Kudos - (**koo**-dohs) - N - fame and renown resulting from an act or achievement - page 187 - chapter 20

Lachrymose - (**lak**-ruh-mohs) - ADJ - given to shedding tears - page 46 - chapter 6

Lackadaisical - (lak-uh-**dey**-zi-kuhl) - ADJ - lacking life, spirit, or zest - page 134 - chapter 14

Lackluster - (**lak**-luhs-ter) - N - lacking liveliness, vitality, spirit, or enthusiasm - page 182 - chapter 19

Lament - (luh-**ment**) - V - to express sorrow, mourning, or regret for often deomstratively - page 156 - chapter 16

Languidly - (**lang**-gwid-ly) - ADV - sluggishly in character or disposition - page 65 - chapter 8

Layman - (**ley**-muhn) - N - a person who does not belong to a particular profession or who is not expert in some field - page 178 - chapter 19

Levity - (**lev**-i-tee) - N - lightness of mind, character, or behavior - page 29 - chapter 4

Liaison - (lee-ey-**zawn**) - N - a person who initiates and maintains a contact or connection between two parties - page 50 - chapter 7

Libel - (**lahy**-buhl) - ADJ - defamation of a person by written or representational means - page 125 - chapter 14

Lionize - (**lahy**-uh-nahyz) - V - to treat as an object of great interest or importance - page 110 - chapter 12

Macerate - (**mas**-uh-reyt) - V - to cause to waste away by or as if by excessive fasting - page 168 - chapter 17

Malodor - (mal-**oh**-der) - N - an offensive odor - page 120 - chapter 13

Meritorious - (mer-i-**tohr**-ee-uhs) - ADJ - deserving praise, reward, esteem, etc. - page 50 - chapter 7

Militate - (**mil**-i-teyt) - V - to have effect or influence; to operate against - page 37 - chapter 5

Mirthful - (**murth**-fuhl) - ADJ - full of gladness or gaiety - page 75 - chapter 9

Modus Operandi - (**moh**-duhs op-uh-**ran**-dahy) - N - distinct pattern or method of operation that indicates or suggests the work of a single criminal in more than one crime - page 152 - chapter 16

Monastic - (muh-**nas**-tik) - ADJ - pertaining to living a secluded life - page 40 - chapter 5

Moniker - (**mon**-i-ker) - N - nickname - page 111 - chapter 12

Myriad - (**mir**-ee-uhd) - N - a great number - page 145 - chapter 15

Nascent - (**nas**-uhnt) - ADJ - having come into existence; developing - page 163 - chapter 17

Nest - (nest) - V - to pack completely together - page 133 - chapter 14

Niggling - (**nig**-ling) - ADJ - petty; bothersome or persistent - page 72 - chapter 9

Nostrum - (**nos**-truhm) - N - a usually questionable remedy, medicine, or scheme - page 98 - chapter 11

Novitiate - (noh-**vish**-ee-it) - N - a beginner in anything; a novice - page 39 - chapter 5

Odious - (**oh**-dee-uhs) - ADJ - arousing or deserving hatred or repugnance - page 146 - chapter 15

Onerous - (**on**-er-uhs) - ADJ - burdensome, oppressive, or troublesome; causing hardship - page 158 - chapter 16

Opulent - (**op**-yuh-luhnt) - ADJ - richly supplied; abundant or plentiful - page 58 - chapter 8

Pacify - (**pas**-uh-fahy) - V - to quiet or calm; to bring to a state of peace - page 154 - chapter 16

Palaver - (puh-**lav**-er) - N - profuse and idle talk - page 62 - chapter 8

Palliative - (**pal**-ee-ey-tiv) - N - something that moderates intensity - page 72 - chapter 9

Panegyric - (pan-i-**jir**-ik) - N - formal or elaborate praise - page 190 - chapter 20

Paradox - (**par**-uh-doks) - N - one (as a person, situation, or action) having seemingly contradictory qualities or phases - page 157 - chapter 16

Parsimonious - (pahr-suh-**moh**-nee-uhs) - ADJ - sparing or frugal - page 44 - chapter 6

Pathos - (**pey**-thos) - N - an emotion of sympathetic pity - page 152 - chapter 16

Pedantic - (puh-**dan**-tik) - ADJ - narrow, and often ostentatiously learned - page 166 - chapter 17

Pejorative - (pi-**jawr**-uh-tiv) - ADJ - tending to disparage or belittle - page 83 - chapter 10

Penance - (**pen**-uhns) - N - a punishment undergone in token of penitence for sin - page 159 - chapter 16

Perquisites - (**pur**-kwuh-zit) - N - things held or claimed as exclusive rights or possessions, informally shortened to "perks" - page 95 - chapter 11

Perturb - (per-**turb**) - V - to disturb greatly in mind - page 66 - chapter 8

Peruse - (puh-**rooz**) - V - read through, as with thoroughness or care - page 51 - chapter 7

Philanthropic - (fil-uhn-**throp**-ik) - ADJ - benevolent; dispensing aid from funds set aside for humanitarian purposes - page 68 - chapter 8

Pique - (peek) - V - to affect with a lively curiosity; to excite - page 56 - chapter 8

Poignant - (**poin**-yuhnt) - ADJ - apt; touching - page 111 - chapter 12

Pontificate - (pon-**tif**-i-keyt) - V - to speak in a pompous manner - page 32 - chapter 4

Porcine - (**pawr**-sahyn) - ADJ - pig-like; hoggish - page 103 - chapter 11

Postmortem - (pohst-**mawr**-tuhm) - ADJ - occurring after death; after the conclusion of an event - page 161 - chapter 17

Potentate - (**poht**-n-teyt) - N - one who wields great power or sway - page 173 - chapter 18

Prattle - (**prat**-l) - N - trifling or empty talk - page 66 - chapter 8

Precarious - (pri-**kair**-ee-uhs) - ADJ - dependent on uncertain premises; dangerous - page 151 - chapter 16

Precept - (**pree**-sept) - N - a command or principle intended especially as a general rule of action - page 157 - chapter 16

Precocious - (pri-**koh**-shuhs) - ADJ - exceptionally advanced in development - page 117 - chapter 13

Presage - (**pres**-ij) - V - to give an omen or warning of - page 135 - chapter 14

Procure - (proh-**kyoor**) - V - to obtain by particular care and effort - page 86 - chapter 10

Profusion - (pruh-**fyoo**-zhuhn) - N - abundance; a great quantity or amount - page 50 - chapter 7

Proletariat - (proh-li-**tair**-ee-uht) - N - the lowest social or economic class of a community - page 173 - chapter 18

Promulgate - (**prom**-uhl-geyt) - V - to make known by open declaration - page 97 - chapter 11

Propinquity - (proh- **ping**-kwi-tee) - N - nearness in place or time - page 66 - chapter 8

Proprietary - (pruh- **prahy**-i-ter-ee) - ADJ - characteristic of an owner - page 32 - chapter 4

Provident - (**prov**-i-dent) - ADJ - frugal - page 121 - chapter 13

Pugnacious - (puhg-**ney**-shuhs) - ADJ - taking pleasure in hostility - page 12 - chapter 1

Puissance - (**pyoo**-uh-suhns) - N - power, might, or force - page 25 - chapter 3

Pulchritude - (**puhl**-kri-tood) - N - beauty; comeliness - page 23 - chapter 3

Pummel - (**puhm**-uhl) - V - to pund; to beat - page 186 - chapter 20

Purvey - (per-**vey**) - V - to supply, usually as a matter of business or service - page 98 - chapter 11

Quaintly - (**kweynt**-lee) - ADV - in a beautifully old-fashioned way - page 14 - chapter 1

Quandary - (**kwon**-dree) - N - a state of perplexity or doubt - page 187 - chapter 20

Quintessential - (kwin-tuh-**sen**-shuhl) - ADJ - the most typical example or representative - page 161 - chapter 17

Quizzically - (**kwiz**-i-kuhlee) - ADV - disbelievingly or
curiously - page 92 - chapter 11

Rancor - (**rang**-ker) - N - bitter deep-seated ill will -
page 155 - chapter 16

Reclusive - (ri-**kloos**-iv) - ADJ - living in seclusion; apart
from society - page 56 - chapter 8

Recondite - (**rek**-uhn-dahyt) - ADJ - dealing with very
profound, difficult, or abstruse subject matter -
page 156 - chapter 16

Redolent - (**red**-l-uhnt) - ADJ - having a pleasant odor;
fragrant - page 24 - chapter 3

Relinquish - (ri-**ling**-kwish) - V - to give up; surrender -
page 22 - chapter 3

Reparation - (rep-uh-**rey**-shuhn) - N - the making fo
amends for wrong or injury done - page 61 -
chapter 8

Replete - (ri- **pleet**) - ADJ - abundantly supplied; full -
page 72 - chapter 9

Repose - (ree- **pohz**) - N - peace or tranquility - page 15 -
chapter 1

Requisite - (**rek**-wuh-zit) - N - essential; necessary -
page 121 - chapter 13

Ruminate - (**roo**-muh-neyt) - V - to go over in the mind
repeatedly and often casually or slowly - page 65 -
chapter 8

Saccharine - (**sak**-er-in) - ADJ - of a sugary sweetness -
page 59 - chapter 8

Sagacious - (suh-**gey**-shuhs) - ADJ - having or showing
acute mental discernment and keen practical sense;
shrewd - page 21 - chapter 3

Salubrious - (suh-**loo**-bree-uhs) - ADJ - favorable to health -
page 44 - chapter 6

Satyric - (**sey**-ter-ic) - ADJ - lecherous; lascivious - page 86 -
chapter 10

Singular - (**sing**-gyuh-ler) - ADJ - extraordinary; odd; distinctive - page 91 - chapter 11

Slough - (sluhf) - V - to cast off - page 127 - chapter 14

Sobriety - (suh-**brahy**-i-tee) - N - the qaulity or state of being sober - page 87 - chapter 10

Soporific - (soh- puh-**rif**-ik) - ADJ - causing or tending to cause sleep - page 11 - chapter 1

Squalid - (**skwawl**-id) - ADJ - marked by filthiness and degradation from neglect or poverty - page 181 - chapter 19

Surfeit - (**sur**-fit) - N - excess - page 43 - chapter 6

Suffuse - (suh-**fyooz**) - V - to spread over or through - page 77 - chapter 9

Sully - (**suhl**-ee) - V - to make soiled or tarnished - page 128 - chapter 14

Superciliously - (soo- per-**sil**-ee-uhs-lee) - ADV - patronizingly haughty - page 141 - chapter 15

Taciturn - (**tas**-i-turn) - ADJ - inclined to silence; quiet - page 23 - chapter 3

Tangential - (tan-**jen**-shuhl) - ADJ - having little relevance - page 162 - chapter 17

Tantamount - (**tan**-tuh-mount) - ADJ - equivalent in value, sigificance, or effect - page 152 - chapter 16

Tawdry - (**taw**-dree) - ADJ - cheap and gaudy in appearance or quality - page 77 - chapter 9

Tepid - (**tep**-id) - ADJ - lacking in passion, force, or zest - page 92 - chapter 11

Terse - (turs) - ADJ - devoid of superfluity; short - page 158 - chapter 16

Threadbare - (**thred**-bair) - ADJ - meager, scanty, or poor - page 40 - chapter 5

Throng - (throng) - N - a crowd - page 55 - chapter 8

Tortuous - (**tawr**- choo-uhs) - ADJ - winding; twisted - page 17 - chapter 2

Turbid - (**tur**-bid) - ADJ - not clear or transparent because of stirred-up sediment or the like; clouded; opaque - page 153 - chapter 16

Unconscionable - (uhn-**kon**-shuh-nuh-buhl) - ADJ - ahockingly unfair or unjust - page 179 - chapter 19

Unremitting - (uhn-ri-**mit**-ing) - ADJ - not stopping or slackening - page 29 - chapter 4

Unrequited - (uhn-ri-**kwahy**-tid) - ADJ - not reciprocated or returned in kind - page 191 - chapter 20

Unsung - (uhn-**suhng**) - ADJ - not celebrated or praised - page 149 - chapter 16

Urbane - (ur-**beyn**) - ADJ - suave; elegant or refined - page 62 - chapter 8

Vagary - (**vey**-guh-ree) - N - an erratic, unpredictable, or extravagant manifestatino, action, or notion - page 99 - chapter 11

Vapid - (**vap**-id) - ADJ - lacking liveliness, tang, briskness, or force - page 166 - chapter 17

Vaunt - (**vawn**-t) - V - to praise or boast about - page 104 - chapter 11

Veneer - (vuh-**neer**) - N - a protective or ornamental facing - page 123 - chapter 13

Veracious - (vuh-**rey**-shuhs) - ADJ - habitually speaking the truth; truthful; honest - page 50 - chapter 7

Verbatim - (ver-**bey**-tim) - ADV - word for word - page 81 - chapter 9

Verdant - (**vur**-dnt) - ADJ - of a green color; inexperienced - page 39 - chapter 5

Vestige - (**ves**-tij) - N - a trace, mark, or visible sign left by something - page 64 - chapter 8

Vie - (vahy) - V - to strive for superiority - 101 - page 11 -

Vitiate - (**vish**-ee-yet) - V - to debase or lower in moral or aesthetic status - page 107 - chapter 12

Vociferous - (voh-**sif**-er-uhs) - ADJ - crying out loudly; clamorous - page 55 - chapter 8

Vogue - (vohg) - N - popular currency, acceptance, or favor; popularity - page 128 - chapter 14

Waft - (waft) - V - to move or go lightly on - page 107 - chapter 12

Wane - (weyn) - V - to dcrease in size, extent, or degree - page 104 - chapter 11

Wanton - (**won**-tn) - ADJ - having no just foundation or provocation - page 153 - chapter 16

Wastrel - (**wey**-struhl) - N - a wasteful person; spend-thrift - page 46 - chapter 6

Woe - (woh) - N - a condition of deep suffering from misfortune, affliction or grief - page 143 - chapter 15

Yen - (yen) - N - strong desire or porpensity - page 99 - chapter 11

Zealously - (**zel**-uhs-lee) - ADV - ardently active, devoted, or diligent - page 38 - chapter 5